SCRATCH WHERE IT ITCHES

SCRATCH WHERE IT ITCHES

Confessions of a Public School Teacher

A Novel

Tony Rotondo

iUniverse, Inc.

New York Lincoln Shanghai

ANTHONY AUGUSTUS
ANGELO

"Do you always talk that way?"

"What way?"

"You know…cussing." He had such a sweet innocent face, the face of an angel. And, God bless 'im, he wanted to be a teacher in the worst way…which is, you know, how most teachers do it.

"I lead two lives, kiddo. One in the classroom and one in real life, and 'whether I shall turn out to be the hero of my own life, or whether that station will be held by anybody else,' only time will tell."

"Isn't that Charles Dickens?" The kid had a sharp ear and was obviously a reader. I liked him instantly. He was one of those junior field observers that local colleges sent to the public schools to give them a whiff of chalk dust and bull shit. I agreed to let him watch me in action twice a week because this was my last year and because nobody else wanted him.

"Why do you want to be a teacher? And don't tell me it's because you love kids. I might think you're a pedophile."

His angelic cheeks reddened. "Why did *you*?"

"I was *called*." He looked at me funny, a tilt of the head like a puppy confused by his master's command.

"You mean from God?"

"No, from Neil Diamond. Of course God! You ever wanted to be a fireman?"

"When I was little, I guess."

"How old are you now?"

"Twenty."

"My *shoes* are twenty…and I never wanted to be anything but a teacher from the day I taught myself to read to right this very minute. *You* have good teachers?"

"Yeah, I guess so."

"You either did or you didn't. There's no *guessing* about it. I have the distinction of having been taught by some of the worst teachers on earth, both public and parochial." The junior field observer lifted his eyebrows. "What's your name?"

"Gary. Gary Phelps." He handed me a folder full of papers. "These are from my supervisor."

"When you're *here*, Gary Phelps, *I* am your supervisor. Got that?"

"Yes sir." He called me *sir*, and he made it sound sincere. The kid was a keeper. You see how starved I was for respect.

"You see, Gary Phelps, I wanted to be a teacher, but not like the ones who took turns beating the shit out of me when I was a kid." I motioned for him to sit down at the desk next to mine. "Did a teacher ever hit you?"

"No, sir. I was a good kid in school." How deliciously naïve Gary Phelps was.

"Do you think that only bad kids get hit in school? Do you think I was a bad kid in school?" He hunched up a shoulder as if to say 'I don't know.'

"Did you ever hit a student?"

"Never. Not once, kiddo." I looked him right in the eye as I moved my old head closer to his young one. "But there are lots of other ways to hurt a kid. Keep your eyes and ears open around here and you'll see." I rifled through his folder. "You live with your parents?"

"Yes sir."

"What do your parents think about your career choice?"

"They're okay with it. Whatever makes me happy."

"If you do it right, Gary, this will make you the happiest guy on earth."

That's what I was—the happiest guy on earth. However, my mother, a child of the Depression, shared neither the Phelps' sentiment nor my euphoria.

"Ma, I want to go to college."

"*Che?*"

"College. I want to be a teacher."

"Teach? You wanna be a teach? *Che patzo!* Gedda job."

People in my family went to high school and then to work. They weren't anti-education as much as they were poor. Not *poor* poor. No food stamps or welfare or anything like that but paycheck to paycheck poor. Everybody had some kind of job both full time and part time. We even did home work. My Uncle Joe…I had three of them…would drop off cases and cases of Reynolds Aluminum Foil labels. They were about four inches wide, the company logo on one side and the postage stamp glue on the other. There were thousands of them in each case. All winter long we'd sit around the huge yellow Formica kitchen table listening to *The Shadow* or *the Long Ranger*…that's what we called him…as we glued the two sides together. They had to be perfectly aligned or my mother would make us trim the edges with her little scissors. I was more into speed than accuracy. I'd slide a label over the damp sponge next to my mile high pile and slap those silver and red babies together. Before I could reach for another, my mother would inspect the fruits of my labor.

"En-doe-knee! *Come brutto*! Nun jew go so fast! Get the siz."

"Ahhh, Ma."

"Nun jew 'Ahhh ma' me! Get the siz…or I get the spoon." We were a family of few words. A couple of them strategically uttered were enough to communicate love, anger, amusement, and threats. I got the 'siz.'

I never knew what those labels got attached to. I just know that for every 100 of them folded in half and glued to perfection, we would earn the princely sum of ten cents.

Some weeks we'd stuff envelopes. We'd fold a yellow flyer extolling the virtues of Fels Naphtha and shove it into a white envelope. Other weeks we'd punch holes in a variety of promotional ads for products that never found their way into our house on Fraley Street. We even did tag team skein rolling of woolen yarn from the factory across the street. It seemed like something a machine could do faster and better, but hey, it brought home money.

"Ma, Antny's makin' it tight," whined my older sister.

"I get the spoon." I loosened up.

Eventually I turned sixteen and branched out and got a real job. Several of them. All founded on lies. I got a job at Food City. Interviewed by Mr. Fishbine, the short, fat, mean, and bald store manager.

"You know how to clean fish?"

"Yes, I do, Mr. Fishbine."

"Okay. Start tomorrow in the fish department…4 to closing."

"Ma, I got a job."

"See? You doan needa go to col *ledge* uh." She stressed the second of three syllables. So did I when I imitated her.

The next day I donned a white apron and a goofy-looking white paper hat, like the kind Nehru wore, and took up my position behind the fish counter.

"May I help you, ma'am?" I was a real charmer with the old ladies.

"Two pounds of flounder, filleted."

I looked in the case. The flounder was in there all right, but in its natural state. The lady wanted it filleted…and I didn't have a clue.

Ira, the fish counter foreman, 'pssted!' me aside: "Hey kid. Grab it by the tail, stick your knife below your thumb and slide your way to the head. See?" I tried it. What I did was a sin. I violated a piscine corpse. That flounder was not filleted, it was shredded. I put Ira's piece on top of my desecration, wrapped it up, and asked the lady if she wanted anything else. She had the good sense to say no.

"You ever clean fish before?" asked the suspicious Ira.

"Sure."

"Sure my Jewish ass." Ira always made it a point to assert his Jewishness. Kind of like Catholics make it a point to assert their Catholicism. I'm a Catholic. See what I mean?

Anyway, I lasted at that job for two years. The Assistant Manager only a few years older than I…I think there was a law passed back in the fifties that remains to this day: Assistant Managers must be between the ages of 17 and 19 because they are the only ones on earth who will take pride in the honorific *Assistant Manager*…was named Tony.

Just about everybody I knew and was related to was named Tony. He got me fired while I was engaged in a scientific experiment. Tony was a smoker and I was just learning how to be one. I had yet to perfect inhaling. In fact I was still working on sophisticated finger-grip. Tony said that people only smoked because they liked to look at the plumes as they left their nose and mouth and curled into the atmosphere above them. He said if you put folks in a completely dark room and gave them cigarettes, they'd quit because they couldn't see the smoke. I told him he was full of shit.

"Okay. I'll prove it to you. Go in the refrigerator and light up." It was a gigantic walk-in with one overhead naked light bulb hanging from the ceiling. It couldn't have been warmer than 35 degrees in there. "Go ahead," urged Tony as he pulled the light chain and shut the door behind him.

The next time it opened it was by Mr. Fishbine. "What the hell are you doing in here?" Thick clouds of smoke swirled about his bald head. "Are you smoking in here?"

"I'm trying to quit."

"You can't quit. You're fired!"

Tony was standing behind him pretending to smoke an invisible cigarette, his hot breath visible in the cold of the refrigerator. He smiled at me as he flicked imaginary ash into his cupped hand. The bastard winked at me.

I also worked in a gas station, a post office, and a bakery. Oh yeah, I was also the student janitor at my high school. Lied there too.

"Know how to ride the mower?

"Yes, Mr. Porchetta, I do."

"Then get out there and cut that grass. Be careful on the bank." Shit! It had a clutch and gears and pedals and it bucked and sputtered until it threw me.

"Sure you can do this?"

"No problem."

"No problem my dago ass!"

Ah! Cultural diversity.

I got to college, not the one I wanted, but the one I could afford. The kids call them safety schools today.

"You work in a post office before?" asked the Post Mistress, who looked like one of the aunts in *Arsenic and Old Lace*.

"Yes, ma'am." Of course I didn't, but I needed the job. I was amazed that college kids actually got mail. I NEVER got any mail at my home except for my Selective Service notification. And nobody ever wrote me at college because I was a commuter.

So I was impressed by all the mail my classmates were receiving daily. Impressed and a little jealous.

I would learn much later in life as a teacher that a good day is an empty mailbox.

My name is Anthony Augustus Angelo. Yeah, Triple A...like I never heard that one before. I went from broken English to English teacher. I went from low class to middle, from poor to comfortable...always shy of well-to-do. But I loved teaching, loved it with a passion, loved it more than money. And that's just how the taxpayers where I lived liked it.

ETERNAL MISERY VS.
PERPETUAL TEARS

"Today, Gary, the surest way for a teacher to lose his job is to touch a kid. Fifty years ago you could hug him, you could shake him, you could yank his hair, you could make him mind. Fifty years ago when you touched a kid, you smacked him upside the head or paddled his butt. Teachers never spared the rod, and there were never many spoiled kids...at least not where I came from. Corporal punishment was expected; hell, it was encouraged. Back then a parent would say to the teacher, 'My kid gives you any lip, *beat* the shit outta him.' Today he says, 'You tap my kid on the shoulder again and my lawyer will *sue* the shit outta ya!'"

Sister Avila Constantine flashed before my eyes. She was my third grade teacher at Our Lady of Eternal Misery. She was IHM...for Immaculate Heart of Mary. And she made us write JMJ on the top of all our papers...Jesus, Mary and Joseph. And we had to leave room on our seats for our Guardian Angel. I swear my sciatica today is directly attributable to that desk sharing. My left cheek was always suspended in unwilling disbelief.

Sister Avila was at least six feet tall. Most of her was always shrouded in black and blue. But the eyebrows to chin exposed to the world revealed a woman mean as hell. She scared the shit out of me. No...worse...she constipated me. I would never ever ask her to go to the lavatory, mainly because she would tell me that I didn't have to go. She knew everything. She was IHM. So I always held it in...and offered it up.

She didn't like me. She didn't like any of us who were Italian. She was Irish and Our Lady of Eternal Misery was an Irish parish with an Irish school. We didn't have a school in my parish, Our Lady of Perpetual Tears. It was all Italian. In this little town there was a church on almost every corner. Our God runneth over. Kids were taught to genuflect and bless themselves every time they passed one. It was perfunctory when no one was looking, but a zealously religious show of piety when adults were in the near occasion of sin.

Up the hill near the park was where we kept the Ukrainians. We called them Ukies. Their golden onion shaped domes gave the town some skyline. We didn't know what went on in there, so we made stuff up. A few blocks away was Our Mother of Sorrows. We were never sure *what* those people were. Across the street was where all the pollacks lived. Their church was Sacred Heart. We used to call it Our Lady of Kielbasa.

My side of the street was all Italian. I lived on the border. Most of the houses were in rows and most of the people worked at Lee's Mill, the carpet maker. My house was right across from Lee's huge parking lot, a mass of concrete surrounded by a ten-foot cyclone fence topped with barbed wire. After my father died of rheumatic fever, my mother, my sister, and I moved in with my aunt, my blind great-grandmother, and my grandfather. My grandfather was a rat bastard. Next to Sister Avila, I feared him most.

My educational experience was quite ecumenical. I got the shit beat out of me in both Catholic and public school. My cheeks, facial and gluteal, were an equal opportunity target for nuns and *laid* teachers alike. That's what we called the ones who weren't nuns.

Sister Avila Constantine, we called her 'ster...we called them all 'ster...was the worst. She made a habit of cowling little kids into submission. She turned tattle-taleing into an art form. She divided and conquered. The bigger she was, the harder we fell.

"Who threw that paper?"

"Antny, 'ster," from the class Judas, Cecilia Bondi. We called her Chi-Chi...but not in class. No nicknames were allowed in class. We all had saints' names and by God we weren't allowed to take them in vain. "Antny did it. I saw him."

There were about forty kids in the class; six of them were Anthonys: Anthony DiSpirito, Anthony Sipriano, Anthony Rapanelli...we called him radish, Anthony Rigatori...of course we called him Rigatoni...Anthony Fecundi...we called him Fuck in Undies, but not in third grade. We didn't learn *fuck* till public school. And there was me, Anthony Augusto Angelo, Triple A.

yers. And every freakin' thing they did wrong would be a manifestation of their disability, anything from telling me to go fuck myself to jacking my jaw.

But I grew to love those kids who then were mostly black, mostly orphans, and mostly illiterate. They supplied me with challenge, hard work, frustration, and a hell of a good time. They were outrageously funny and disarmingly frank.

"Mr. Angelo, do you make adjustments for different learning styles?"

"What?" I knew I sounded annoyed which defeated the purpose of my telling Gary to feel free to ask me questions about anything.

"Learning styles. Multiple intelligences. Individual differences?"

I was nonplussed by his question. I tried to frame my answer in the most professional way I could. "Those kids that just left here are labeled Academic. Back in the day they would have been labeled slow learners. I'm sure you're familiar with the textbook definitions and descriptions of slow learners—from Jencks to Holt—which are scholarly as well as maudlin. Here's what I found, Gary. A slow learner is a kid who will fart out loud and scratch where it itches. I have found also that I.Q. is inversely proportional to the volume of the fart and the location of the itch." Gary pretended to write that down in his notebook. I smiled and tapped his book as if to say get this down too. "Observe if you will a student of above-average intelligence. He is plagued by gastric inhibitions. He would rather burst than blast. He has never laid a public fart. Have you?"

It was now Gary's turn to be nonplussed. I took his silence for acquiescence. "I can remember one of mine in high school, at a basketball game, I think. I let one in a fairly close crowd and quickly turned to the kid behind me saying 'Geez!' and shot him a look of fartless disgust. Above-average kids don't do stuff like that. And talk about scratching. Smart kids pretend to have only itchy noses. But when no one is looking, they're groin-grabbers like the rest of us. They're nose pickers too. That *average* kid that sat in front of you this morning is a social climber. Did you see him? He held his book up in front of his face and damn near pulled his eye through his nostril. But that's the difference, Gary. Slow learners pick out in the open. And if you catch them, they smile at you. How many smart kids do you know who would do that?"

"Seven." *I* pretended to write that down. Then he read from his college notes, "When Gardner interacted with Csikszentmihalyi and Feldman, he understood that intelligence is a biological and psychological potential; that potential is capable of being realized to a greater or lesser extent as a consequence of the experiential, cultural, and motivational factors that affect a person." He drew a circle around the paragraph slicing through it with a diagonal slash. He wrote Scratch Where It Itches in the margin and smiled. The kid had a sense of humor.

I rolled my rickety old chair to my old battleship-gray filing cabinet and searched for the source of Gary's note. "Listen to this, Gar. 'We cannot assume that *style* means the same thing to Carl Jung, Jerome Kagan, Tony Gregoric, Bernice McCarthy, and other inventors of stylistic terminology. There is little authority for assuming that an individual who evinces a style in one milieu or with one content will necessarily do so with other diverse contents-and even less authority for equating styles with intelligences.'" Then I showed him how *I* had circled and slashed it. He laughed when he saw that I had written Bullshit! in the margin. I felt like adopting him.

I remember one time I was carrying myself aloft with a lecture on the Victorian Age. And in my Dickensian enthusiasm some scholarly spittle lighted on the hand of the kid sitting in front of me. I saw it leave my mouth and settle on his unsuspecting wrist. He saw it too. But he did nothing about it. You looked at him and you knew he wanted to wipe it off fast as hell. But he wouldn't because I purposely kept eye contact, and I guess no smart kid wants to hurt the teacher's feelings by rubbing off his spit while he's looking.

But you take a slow learner. He'll tell you to "Say it, don't spray it!" and wipe it off on *your* sleeve. This to me is normal behavior. To too many other teachers and to most administrators though, this is insolence.

I must have been a slow learner too because most administrators thought I was insolent. This is not to suggest that I openly farted and scratched, but that I possessed a proclivity to engage in unadulterated veracity. If the truth had to be told…like there was spinach between your teeth, or your tie didn't match your suit, or the Emperor was naked, I was the one to do it.

This calling often got me in trouble. And I often blamed Jesus.

the corner from my street anyway. There had been a terrible airplane crash that killed most passengers. One who survived was the grandson of the Frachettis, our around the corner neighbors. He suffered third degree burns over 70% of his body. His hands and face were badly disfigured. His parents and brother and sister died in the crash. He loved Gene Autry and Gene Autry heard about it so he came to town…with Champion. When the neighborhood kids got wind of it, we swarmed around the row house and the horse trailer that housed the magnificent steed. I don't know how Gene got there. He just materialized before our young and gawking eyes. The Frachetti boy, still bandaged from months of skin grafts, was wheeled outside to meet his hero and his horse. Flash bulbs popped as the local newspaper and all the kids' parents took a gazillion pictures. I don't remember if Gene said anything. He must have. All I remember is he was there, live, right in front of me. I touched his horse. The only other *star* I ever touched was John Fitzgerald Kennedy years later when he drove through our town on his way to make a speech someplace else.

I never thought to ask Gene Autry for an autograph, but later that night when everybody had gone home leaving the Frachettis alone in their fleeting celebrity and lasting grief, I scooped up some Champion horseshit, put it in a brown lunch bag, and took it home.

No magazines came to our house. And the newspaper was only delivered on Sundays. I read it all, even the ads. I don't remember any books being in the house when I was a kid. I have no memory of my mother reading me bedtime stories or making up ones of her own. Most nights she'd sit in her chair closest the TV because she was hard of hearing. I'd lie on the floor at her feet perpendicular to the set and only inches away from the dials so I could change the channel, increase the volume, and shut it off. All, of course, at Borzoni's direction. My mother usually fell asleep at the beginning of one program and would wake up at the end of another. She never knew what the hell was going on. She often fell asleep with her mouth open and on occasion I would slip one or two of Borzoni's *Salaam* cigarettes in there.

My mother had a tough life. She worked hard morning to night and when she sat down to a little TV, sleep washed over her, fortifying her for yet another day of tedium. At the time I felt cheated of her attention, but now I do the same thing. I have no clue how any program ends.

I vowed that when I was married and had kids of my own, we would eat in the dining room loaded with lots of matching dishes, an arsenal of knives, forks, and spoons, and scintillating conversation that would shed light on the national and international scene. I broke my vows in 1980. That's when we added a TV to the kitchen.

To speak of deprivation is to invite thoughts of malnutrition or starvation. Such was not the case. I was well fed on a steady diet of starches and carbohydrates then as I was fed on a steady diet of baloney and American cheese now. I never saw or ate a shrimp until I was twenty. Never had a steak all to myself. Never had *antipasto, prosciutto e melone, alfredo, carbonara*. Never ate out. By comparison my ten-year old grandson orders sushi in Thai restaurants. See? That kid is not deprived. He already knows that you eat the salad before the entrée. When I was his age, I didn't even know what an entrée was.

Red gravy was poured over most things and hunks of thick-crusted Italian bread would sop it all up. It's what I knew. It's what I ate. And what I ate made me ordinary.

One time I took my wife to one of those restaurants that have three dollar signs after its name in the Entertainment book; you know, buy one at the regular price and get the second one free? After the high-priced meal was over, I ordered a cup of tea. The waiter brought over a wooden chest, flipped open the lid, and tilted its contents toward me. It was loaded with teas, foreign and domestic. The waiter suggested chamomile but I opted for Lipton. *That's* ordinary.

Nobody ever asked what my school day was like when I was a kid. My mother didn't have a clue about my school life. Early on I learned how to forge her name so she never saw report cards, health cards, or any other cards the school sent home. She assumed I was well behaved, courteous and obedient to the Sisters of the Immaculate Heart of Mary. She assumed I knew I would burn in hell if I wasn't.

I imagine there are lots of kids out there even in this modern day and age who are strangers to their parents…and vice versa. Lots of the kids I've taught had no clue what their parents did for a living. My own son had no idea I was a teacher. He thought I just marked papers at the kitchen table. At least that's what he told the folks who tested him for kindergarten. They let him in anyway. But I've progressed. I've moved on. I've learned things, been places. Hey! I've seen *Aida* at the Met!

But everywhere I am burdened with the common touch. My ordinariness is often at odds with the extraordinariness of things and places I have encountered later in life. I've visited museums from Philadelphia to Vatican City, but I buy paintings to match my couch. I smuggle cheap candy and soda into expensive Broadway theaters. I eat only in restaurants where salads and vegetables are included. A la carte is anathema to me.

Television brought the universe into my limited world. As I lay on the woven straw carpet of green and white braids that left their mark on my young butt and legs, I saw things that reinforced the shabbiness of my surroundings. I can still see my mother trying to keep the place clean. She had fashioned a sprinkler from an old 7Up bottle which she fitted with a wine cork stabbed full of holes. She would sprinkle water over the straw carpet to cut down on dust and then sweep the rug into submission. She made me do the baseboards every week. I swirled an old rag into a bucket of water and Lysol. It smelled just like the school lavatory of Our Lady of Eternal Misery. The good sisters there often had class miscreants clean the pee-stained floors. If you were especially bad or if the sisters were feeling especially mean, you were made to scrub the urinals as well. If you were lucky enough to be punished with a friend, you could have a hockey game with the deodorizing pink puck that covered the drain. If you won the toss, you got to use the broom. If you lost, you got the mop. Ever try to hit anything with a wet mop? It can be done, but not with precision. Neither could cleaning the baseboards in my *palor*. The bare floors were not flush. Some were splintered and would snag my rag and prick my fingers. Always there were mouse droppings under the radiators. Some nights the little critters scampered right by my legs as I watched *I Love Lucy*. Some times they came out in the daylight. We often pretended that we didn't see them. I was put in charge of traps. But no matter how many I snared, reinforcements always showed up the very next night. I never asked friends to come over for fear the mice would come as well.

The things I could only imagine from the radio were now snowy black and white pictures on television. One of my uncle Joes worked for a novelty company that sold inexpensive junk to suckers like the Angelos. My mother bought a sheet of cellophane to place over the TV. It was blue at the top, red in the middle, and green at the bottom. Voila! Color TV. At least that's what we pretended.

I loved everything about television. I still do. So does my wife. And my kids. Individually and collectively we do not trust folks who do not like TV. We are suspicious of those who say they do not watch it. We are shocked to learn that some don't even have one. If we could afford it, we'd have one in every room. So would all other ordinary people. TV is the ordinary guy's window on the world. Always was. Always will be. World without end. Amen.

How's that for *zeitgeist*? (I just threw that in in case you were an *extraordinary* reader.)

The cosmopolitan Gary Phelps thanked both his parents for encouraging him to write stories and poetry. He concluded with "I want to share my love of learning, in particular, my love of language with young adults. I want them to experience the power of words."

Wow! I could never write anything like that, not and be telling the truth. Although I can't remember what I put on my *dossier* forty-five years ago, it was probably something I thought was funny. The truth hurt too much.

"Oh, *Jesu Cristo mia!* Oh, *Madonna mia! Mi fa male la testa! Fa malae la gamba; fa male lo stomaco! Oh, Jesu!*" Once every six months or so Gennaro Borzoni would take to his bed and cry out to the saints that he was going to die. He was my mother's father, the rat bastard I lived with after my father died of rheumatic fever.

Borzoni, that's what the town called him, never looked sick a day in his life. Even on the day he finally did die, he looked pretty healthy to me. Ah! But could he act! He was like one of those old time impressionists who would look at you with their own faces, make a quick 180, and present one totally different...like Jimmy Durante. (He was the patron saint of comedians in my neighborhood.)

Borzoni had twelve kids, but only eight made it to adulthood. His wife Assunta was long dead before I moved in with him. There's only one picture of her that I've ever seen. She's sitting on a pile of cinder blocks with her elbow on one of them, her open hand against her head. She has a Mona Lisa smile and a hair net. She'd look good on a can of tomato paste. All her kids said she went to heaven and they all cursed Borzoni for sending her there well before her time.

The five daughters and three sons were not so crazy about the Old Man. That's what they all called him. Pop to his face, Old Man to each other. So after they married they moved as far away as they could afford...the next town over, usually. Now Borzoni craved attention. He wanted his kids and grandkids...especially those who bore his name...to come see him regularly, every Sunday afternoon, in fact. All of them. Every Sunday. But sometimes they didn't come. And after they missed a week, the second was easier, the third a breeze. But if you missed four, Borzoni took to his bed and began the dying process.

"*Oh Jesu! Mi fa male...ahhh!*" When no one ran to his room at the top of the stairs, he cranked up the volume. "*AHHHHHH! Jesu! Madonna MIA!*" Aunt Rosalie, who slept in the middle room with my blind great-grandmother, was the first on the death scene.

"Wus wrong, Pop?" It was hard to understand Aunt Ro early in the morning. See, she was a little plump, most of the fat lodged in her chins. So she wore a chinstrap to bed thinking that the fat would be forced into her soft palate or great-grandmother was asked by the great-grandchild WHY, it was explained that the meat wouldn't fit in her pot.

We went to church every Sunday without fail. We never had a car so we walked the proverbial mile in the snow. If we complained about the distance or the cold, we were told to offer it up. In my neighborhood the more devout, the earlier the mass. Of course we went to the 7:30. Not only did we get a Latin mass, we got a bonus sermon in Italian. Perpetual Tears was too far away for Great-grandmom Carmella so she was exempt. She kept holy the Sabbath in her own way and since she couldn't see, that usually involved setting something on fire. She was convinced her prayers were futile unless accompanied by dripping wax. One Christmas the Old Man gave her a plaster of Paris altar the size of a two-slice toaster. It had three rows of plastic candles that lit up when you turned the base. No matches required. She worshipped it...literally. Flanked by foot-high statues of Jesus...from birth to death to resurrection...St. Anthony, St. Theresa, some others I couldn't name, and the Blessed Mother...she had all her bases covered from sickness to death to lost articles. Sometimes she would stand the Blessed mother on her head in the *palor* to dispel bad weather. For severe thunder and lightning storms, she would thrust a hatchet into the ground and pray to St. Barbara that lightning would pass over the house and strike the pollacks across the street.

I was Great-grandmom's seeing eye dog. It was my job to 'go get her and bringer'...that was the order my mother always gave me. "En-doe-knee! Go get your granmud and bringer to the table." I could never figure out how she got to the places where I 'fetched' her without my help. I often harbored the suspicion that she wasn't really blind at all, and to that end I would occasionally test her. At least once a month I would sneak into her sanctuary and rearrange her statues. And every month they'd all be back in their 'right' places. Sometimes I'd move furniture, but she never walked into any.

I remember one day Great-grandmom came out the back door, walked down two steps to the cement slab that separated the house from the side yard where her tomato and pepper plants basked in the sun. She had an old kitchen chair out there right in the middle of the garden and she liked sitting there just fingering her rosary beads and enjoying the warmth of a cloudless day.

I followed her...stalked her really. When she finally got herself all comfortable and was deep into her second decade, I pulled out my water pistol, aimed at the sky over her head, and squeezed the trigger. *"Che? Piove? C'e il sole!"* She must have thought it was a miracle...raining on a sunny day. I quietly laughed my ass off as she got up and slowly made her way back to the house, raindrops falling on her head. She went inside while I reloaded and staked out the door. Sure enough Great-grandmom showed up to check on the weather conditions. She opened the screen door and stuck her hand out, palm up. My shot was perfect. It arced up and then down and splattered on her. She retreated back inside…I guessed to turn the Blessed Mother on her head.

One other time that I shadowed her around was a lesson in anatomy that I was not ready to learn. She had walked over to the rickety wooden fence that supported rose bushes whose fragrance always drew her like a magnet. I watched as she breathed in the flowers she loved but couldn't see. That's when I heard the water dripping. Great-grandmom was peeing…right out there in the yard…standing up. I was amazed. How did she do it? And without wetting her dress! I got down on my knees and looked up her dress. The expression "Gross me out!" was born.

I could be as blind as Great-grandmom and still know I was in Perpetual Tears. The candles, the incense, and the old ladies…all gave off an unforgettable aroma, pungent but not unpleasant. My mother bobby-pinned a black lace handkerchief to her hair. It was a sin in those days for women to be uncovered. She went to the ladies' side after signing in. That's what we used to call dipping our fingers in the holy water and blessing ourselves when entering. Sometimes we'd genuflect for full effect, an outward and ostentatious show of our faith. Even though I was only about ten, I insisted on sitting on the men's side. That's where some of the older boys in the neighborhood sat. Before we separated, my mother wagged her finger at me and twisted her lips counterclockwise. It was the unspoken threat of the wooden spoon if I misbehaved.

Salvatore was the worst. Sitting next to him guaranteed a beating later that night. He always said or did something to make the rest of us laugh. None of us knew Latin but we had heard the expressions so many times that we knew when the priest, Father Testa…you could probably guess what we called him…intoned one or the other to stand or kneel or beat our breasts.

Salvatore liked to be the first to stand. We would often follow his lead…and be the only ones in the congregation to do so. When the bells rang…we never knew why…he beat his breast so hard you could hear it three pews back. When the priest said, "*Dominus vobiscum*" Salvatore simultaneously prayed "Dominic, go frisk them"…just as the collection basket passed before us. All the kids were given 50 cents to offer up. Salvatore always dipped in for change.

When the priest got to "*Et cum spiritu tuo,*" Salvatore would say, "Here comes Billy DiSpirito too." Billy would always try to fart when he said it. At the end of the mass Father Testa would say: "Savior of the world…" to which we were sup-

Keeping Holy the Sabbath

The Freewrites were always the best part of the class. The kids loved to share, especially when the subject was controversial. They would rant and rave at each other when abortion sides were taken or capital punishment or the drinking age or the legalization of marijuana. My job was to select a subject that could lead into the literature mandated by our school district. Sometimes it was seamless. Other times it was cheesy. I knew because the kids would groan and yell, "Cheesy!"

"We're going to read *The Scarlet Letter* next week. Any ideas for a Freewrite topic?" Gary looked surprised that I asked him. And well he should be. We old-timers rarely asked the new teachers for help or advice. The notable exception is in the area of technology. Stuff like "Could you show me how to attach a document to my email?"

"How about Secrets," said Gary.

"Good one. How about you write it on the board today?"

"For real?!"

"Don't get on my nerves, Gar. For real! Now get in there."

He tightened the knot in his tie. I insisted on professional dress. A tie was mandatory, a jacket was optional. Most of my male colleagues looked like they worked in the automotive department of Sears. On Friday Dress Down Days you couldn't tell the difference. I wore suits, the best my meager salary could supply. Often it was buy one, get one free. I had a different tie for every school day of the year. If I could have afforded it, I would have worn a tuxedo to class to show the kids how important I thought it and they were.

Gary was looking fine as he strode into the room booming "Good morning!" The class smiled and boomed right back.

"Today's Freewrite is Secrets. Take five quiet minutes to jot your thoughts down."

"He sounds like you, Mr. Angelo." I blushed. This junior field observer was going places.

The kids shared their *friends'* secrets and called on Gary to share his. This is what he said. "Somewhere in China there's a diminishing number of little old ladies who communicate through a secret script called *nushu*. They share their joys, sorrows, hopes, and fears in a secret language unknown to the men around them." As the cheesy saying goes, the silence was deafening.

"Good one, Mr. Phelps. Let's take a closer look at these two words." I wrote *Secret Script* on the board. "Do any of you have a secret script?" Of course they did and were quick to fill the board with lol, pig Latin, and slang relative to sex and drugs. "Well, Mr. Phelps, we're wondering what all this has to do with *The Scarlet Letter*." We all turned to watch him turn crimson, a shade most complementary to his tie.

"Based on what we've heard in here, we all have secrets, we all know secrets, and we all know how hard it is to keep secrets. Keep in mind what we shared with each other as we learn about the secrets Hawthorne's characters hide from each other. And as we read, ask yourself: would I tell?" Gary caught my eye just as I winked it. I thought, 'Quite a save, young man, quite a save.'

Like those little old Chinese ladies, Borzoni's family had its own language. Most of it was centered around food. It's how we kids learned about body parts and sex. Nobody ever gave us *the talk*; we just paid careful attention at the kitchen table and learned all we needed to know to be reproductive, contributing members of society. That's what I wrote about.

"Did you see the watermelons on that? *Maddona mia!*" Uncle Amerigo...at the table we called him something that sounded like 'zio mah eeg'...held his hands out in front of him as though he were weighing two basketballs. He was ogling a picture of Jayne Mansfield. "I wouldn't mind burying my salami in that."

"Weiner, you mean." Uncle Joe held up his thumb and index finger a scant two inches apart.

"Watch your language. There's kids here." Aunt Lizzie was sensitive to our virgin ears. "These are called bazooms." She cupped her breasts. Well, she tried to. They were quite prodigous. In fact they *WERE* watermelons. "And this is your goozie." She squeezed her rear end.

"And this," added Uncle Sal clutching his crotch, "is your *braciola*." He was the husband Aunt Lizzie out-weighed by 100 pounds.

'Tommy-toodle," corrected Aunt Lizzie. "That's your Tommy-toodle. And leave it alone."

So it went on the Sundays when all the aunts and uncles and cousins would show up to visit Borzoni. All the aunts brought a cake or a pie. The uncles went to the Polish deli and brought back lunchmeats, cheeses, and rolls. They called the deli The Pollack's. They called the dry goods store The Jew's. Not name-calling, just names they were called. That's what we kids thought anyway.

"Hey Liz! Did Sal help you fill your cannolis?" Zio Mah Eeg was unrelenting. He reached over and poked Uncle Sal in the ribs, just lightly, but it was enough to make Sal jump out of his chair and babble a bilingual string of nonsense and profanity. Sal was what they called goosey. Touch him anywhere unexpectedly and he would lose control for three or four seconds. We kids never touched him. Just Mah Eeg. One time he did it when Uncle Sal was eating a meatball and he almost choked to death.

Are you getting an idea of how my values were shaped? My sister was the oldest of all the grandchildren. That meant she could sit at the table…if there was room. Most of the time she just bossed all the other kids around. And if we didn't do what she said, she told on us. From the kitchen we'd hear: "En-do-knee! Frankie! David! Theresa Ann! Lydia! Remo! Eva! Suzanne! Marie!" We never heard Gennaro's name called out. He was named after Borzoni and his shit didn't stink. But for the rest of us, just hearing our names was supposed to make us stop whatever we were doing. The older we got, the less effective that particular method. By the time we hit double digits, we responded only to wooden spoons and leather belts.

They all showed up at the same time—4:30. In fact, if some came earlier, they would sit out in their cars and wait until the others appeared. Nobody wanted one-on-one time with Borzoni. They all brought their specialty, all except Aunt Jule. She didn't bring anything. Everybody called her a bitch…behind her back. She didn't give a shit. She said she had more important things to do on a Sunday than sit around a dirty kitchen watching Uncle Sal choke on meatballs.

Aunt Theresa never made anything but pineapple upside down cake. My mother made what everyone called pound and a half cake because it was so heavy.

Aunt Lizzie made cannolis with enough rum to make the weekly visit bearable. Aunt Rosalie made pizzeles with an iron on loan from the Smithsonian. She had to hold one of the long handles against her forehead as she spooned the batter. When she closed it, she said half a Hail Mary. When she got to Holy Mary, Mother of God, she flipped the iron over. The hotter the iron got, the faster she prayed. Aunt Jenny brought pumpkin pie...no matter the season. Aunt Lil brought fruit. Everybody thought she was stuck up.

Everybody left at the same time so nobody could talk trash about them. That's how my family kept holy the Sabbath.

"NAVY blue," I said.

"Shud uppa!" I forgot the unspoken rule: Borzoni does ALL the talking. "How much thisa?" He lifted a sleeve from the rack.

"That's black." Borzoni shot me a look that could freeze blood.

The salesman said that these suits were for kids and that I needed a bigger size. He said it loud. My grandfather said, "Hey! He's a kid!"…louder.

"Let me show you these in the back."

"Gonna cost more in the backa? Nun jew jack uppa da price or I go crossa da street."

"He needs a men's size."

"*Che* men? He'sa ten years olda!" Other customers turned to see.

"He's a big boy. Needs room in the seat, and the shoulders. Let's try one on." I slid my arm into a suit jacket. It was not navy blue but I was keeping that to myself. The sleeves covered all but my fingertips.

"*Quanto costa*…how much dissa?" Oooh! A Borzoni slip. He spoke Italian, a no-no in the haggling process with a Jew. He thought his English was perfect and that he had no detectable accent. He believed that they…the Jews…would raise the price if you sounded foreign.

"Let's try on the pants."

"How mucha?"

"Behind that curtain, young man."

"Che younga man! He's a *kid*! How mucha?"

I came out from behind the curtain. The pants fit around the waist, a whopping size 36. I had to roll them up two or three times.

"We can shorten those sleeves and the pants. Nice, huh?" It wasn't nice and it wasn't navy blue.

"I'ma looka some more," said Borzoni in *flawless* English. He walked from rack to rack, touching some, shunning others. The salesman followed close behind pointing out one stylish number after another. I knew where we were headed. **CLEARANCE**. The big red sign pulled my grandfather like a magnet. "En-doe-knee, finda one. *Andiamo*! Hurry uppa!"

I made one quick lap around the closeout rack. They were all blue but none said NAVY blue. I was worried that it would be the wrong shade and that would piss off Sister Avila who would heap scorn on me for embarrassing the visiting confirming bishop. "Atsa da one?"

"Yes." I really had no choice.

"Fifteen dollar," offered Borzoni.

"$29.99," countered the salesman.

"Sixteen dollar or I go crossa da street," said my grandfather as he grabbed my arm and pulled me to the front.

"Hold on. Hold on. Across the street doesn't have quality like this." The salesman held up my arm to illustrate the workmanship. "You're a tailor. You know good stuff when you see it."

"Sixteen dollar."

We were at the front door and I was still wearing the suit with the rolled up pants.

"You drive a hard bargain, Mr. Borzoni." This was the store's owner. He knew Borzoni by name. "Every year I think I'm going to get full price, and every year you steal my profit away. I'm just glad I don't have too many other customers like you. Okay, okay, sixteen dollars."

While I changed, Borzoni paid. As we went out the door my grandfather, ever sensitive to others said, "*Buona Pasqua!* Happy Easter."

I can't be sure but I think the salesman outside mumbled "Goddamn dagos!" as we wended our way home.

That sixth grade year was a turning point in my life. That's when the stock market crashed. Not THE stock market, just the Angelo Stock Market on my street. My mother was laid off. The hand sewers were being replaced with machines. Tuition was going to double so it was decided that my sister and I would go public. It was the answer to my prayers, the novena that never fails finally paid off. I feigned disappointment. My mother told me to offer it up. I did…with a secret smile.

The kids on the corner were talking excitedly about Boy Scouts. Perpetual Tears was going to sponsor a troop. We all went to the organizational meeting in the church basement. One of the fathers talked about scouting and all the fun we'd have and all the places we'd go. We'd even camp out overnight. He passed out permission slips and told us to return them signed by next week's meeting. I read the notice on the way home. Not only did I have to return a signed form, I also had to include five dollars for annual membership. I tore it up and created a sour grapes story to tell my mother.

"You gonna be boy scouta?"

"Nah. I don't want to sleep outside on the ground."

When spring rolled around, some of the neighborhood fathers thought it would be a good idea to start a Little League team. We all went to the organizational meeting at the park. This sounded as good as the Boy Scouts. We'd be called the Phillies and we'd be sponsored by Green's Drugstore. We'd have red shirts with white letters and numbers. All we had to have was our own glove. See? There was always a catch.

"You gonna play basea ball?"

"You need a glove."

"How mucha?"

"I don't know but I don't think I want to play anyway." She knew I was lying. I kept a scrapbook of the Phillies, anything and everything about them down to the box scores. It wasn't a real scrapbook, just sheets of paper I took home from school. One side was filled with names of companies who donated their discarded stationery to the school to cut down on paper expenses. I never saw a blank piece of paper the whole time I went to that school.

"Nun jew worry," said my mother.

She had signed up for unemployment but was looking for another job in the meantime. She found one in Woolworth's Five and Ten. I never knew exactly what she did there but I knew she got a discount.

"En-doe-knee, you gonna play basea ball?"

"Nah."

"What ahm gonna do with this glovea then?" She held it out to me. My stomach dropped, my eyeballs popped. "Nicea, huh?"

"Yeah, Ma, nice. Thanks." I took it and ran to my room. It was a little kid's glove. The kind you wear when you *pretend* to play baseball. I couldn't even fit my hand in it. The price tag was still on it...$1.99...less her discount. I'd be laughed off the field if I took that to practice. And I would hurt her feelings if I told her it was the wrong kind of glove. So I lied. I pretended to go up the park with my pretend glove in my back pocket. It was actually small enough to fit. I told one of the guys to tell his father that I had to help out at home and couldn't play on the team. I told my mother that I was cut.

"Cut?! You needa ban-dage? Come on. I fix."

"No, Ma. Cut means you're not good enough to play on the team."

"Who says you no good enough? I fix him too. And you gotta nicea glove too," she added.

"Maybe you can get your money back," I said. "The tag is still on it."

I survived that lean year. I made my Confirmation and my first adult decision by picking my uncle Gus to be my sponsor. Sister Avila announced to me and the class that *Gus* was not a saint and that I had to pick someone else. I told my mother who explained to me that Gus was short for Augusto. Who knew? I had a great aunt named Angeline. I thought her name was Sissy because all the adults called her Sissy Angeline. I was surprised to learn that what I heard as Sissy was ziz-zee, a corruption of *zia*…aunt. Again, who knew?

When my grandfather heard that I picked Uncle Gus for my sponsor and that I would take his name for my middle name, he went off into an apoplectic fit. He hated Gus from the first time his daughter Jennie brought him to the house. "Montenegro? Siciliano? Mafioso!" Borzoni was from Abruzzi and thought that anyone south of there was low life. I didn't know that either.

My Confirmation Day was quite an event. I was decked out in my new blue suit, not navy but Sister Avila said she'd put me at the end of the procession and I'd walk alone so no one would notice. I had broken in the suit on Easter Sunday. My mother did the alterations herself but couldn't bring herself to actually cut the fabric so she merely hemmed the sleeves and cuffs. It looked like I was wearing mufflers and shin guards.

Borzoni refused to attend the mass, but that was no big deal since he had excommunicated himself years ago when his mother died. He was good at holding grudges both against God and Sicilians.

We were all scared to death that the Bishop would ask us hard questions and that he would slap us hard if we screwed up. It was Sister who shared both scenarios with us as she terrified us through our daily drills. One of her favorites was "How many mothers do you have?" It was too easy so we all knew there was a trick up her long black sleeve. We all knew except Antoinette. She was slow. She'd be learning support today. Not knowing her ass from her elbow was a manifestation of her disability.

"One, 'ster."

"Stand up!" yelled Sister.

"One!" yelled Antoinette as she stood at attention smiling her vacuous smile.

"Wrong!"

"Two!"

"Wrong! Wrong! Wrong!"

Antoinette was beside herself. She teared up and blurted out "Seven!" We laughed but when Sister hit her we stopped abruptly.

"We'll stay here all day if we have to, Antoinette. Now how many mothers do you have?" Sister's eyes bore into Antoinette's and she did the unthinkable. She wet herself. I was glad she was no relative of mine. Not because she was slow but because relatives were always called upon for clean up. Her cousin Carmen was sent for the mop.

"At least she didn't throw up this time," I whispered to him on his way out.

"I have three mothers, Sister. My mother who gave me birth, the Blessed Virgin Mary, Mother of God, and our holy mother the Church," said Chi-Chi who always tried to curry favor with Sister but rarely succeeded.

"No one called on you, Cecilia. Five Hail Marys…on your knees." Chi-Chi was right but her only reward would be in heaven.

I was the last to be confirmed and the last to leave the church. The original plan was to go back to my house for cake and coffee but Aunt Jennie was afraid the Old Man would start a fight with her husband. Uncle Gus shook my hand and placed an envelope in my pocket. Then he and Aunt Jennie drove off. My mother, sister, and I walked home, stopping at Green's Drugstore for a cherry coke. That was my party. My sister told me to open the envelope. Inside were a holy card and a scapular.

Adulthood sucked.

On Gary's last day with me we celebrated with piles of junk food and generic colas. I always fed my students great quantities of very cheap comestibles on special occasions, and this was one of them. The kids made cards, especially the girls. One sweet young thing with limited resources wrote simply:

Phelps helps…me!!!!!

They were going to miss him. So was I.

"You give me faith, kid. You're going to be a great teacher."

"Thanks. But I don't think so."

"Of course you are. Trust me. I know these things."

"I decided I want to be a writer." I was thinking *Che writer! Be a teach!* But I learned long ago never to piss on someone else's dream. I once told a kid that the attractive covers he made for all his essays were nice but he needed to spend more time on his writing and less on his drawing. Today that kid's oils of landscapes sell for over $20,000 per attractive cover.

"You'll be a great writer." But I know I didn't sound very enthusiastic. I was hurt. I was crushed. This kid was like a son to me. What a loss to the kids! All right. What a loss to me!

"Don't you want to know why?"

"Well, I know it's not the money." We both smiled. "And I know it's not the kids." His smile broadened.

"It's *you*. You make it all look so easy and so much fun, but I've seen you after hours and at all those IEP meetings. There's too much politics and resistance. You can joke about it but I don't think I can."

"In 1964 I joined a teachers' union. In fact, I was a charter member even before I had tenure. I think administrators then construed that as slow learner insolence, but today it would be construed as a manifestation of my disability."

"Ah," said Gary, "then you'd be entitled to learning support." See why I liked this kid?

"Now there's an itch sorely in need of scratching…learning support. Maybe you should write about that. Taxpayers are forking over millions of dollars to supply kids with private school education in the neighborhood public school."

"Is this going to be a speech?"

I ignored him. "Lawyers and other self-proclaimed child advocates have invaded the campus and taken the administrators hostage."

"Sounds like a speech, Mr. Angelo."

"I used to tell parents their kids were lazy, less-than-gifted pains in the neck to me and their peers. And parents would apologize and straighten their kids out. They were the good ol' days of common sense and plain talk."

"See? That's what I don't want any part of."

"What? Common sense and plain talk? Ambiguous modification, Gar.

"Watch it."

But the kid was right. My last ten years in this forty-year odyssey between Scylla and Charydis were plagued with Individual Educational Plan (IEP) meetings where jargon was rife and sanity was gone with the wind. No English was spoken, just acronyms and prepositions. The Individuals with Disabilities Education Act (IDEA) legislated schooling meted out in the Least Restricted Environment (LRE). Instructional Support Teams (IST's) were formed and tests were given up the wazoo.

One of my doozies had Attention Deficit Disorder (ADD)…the disability of choice in affluent neighborhoods. Plus he had a mouth like a drunken sailor on leave. Everything was "fuck this" or "fuck that" with this kid. I thought he was rude and disrespectful. Dumb ass me. Little did I know that he needed a FUBA…Functional Behavioral Assessment so that his CER…Comprehensive Evaluation Report…could pinpoint his SLD…Specific Learning Disorder. His SDI…Specially Designed Instruction…mandated LS…Learning Support to implement his BMP…Behavior Management Plan. Here's how it worked:

"Dward (not his real name; that would be a FERPA [Family Educational Rights and Privacy Act] violation), would you please keep your eyes on your own paper?" He tended to rely heavily on the work of others.

"Fuck that."

"Pardon me?"

"Fuck that. What are ya, deaf?"

"Dward, let's take a deep breath and count to ten. One, two, three…"

"Fuck you!"

"…four, five, six…" When I got to ten I was to call the Intervention Specialist who was trained in Anger Management and Restraint. "I'm sending Dward to you…Yes, three times…Yes, that *is* down four from yesterday…Well, loud enough for the class to hear…No, I didn't encourage him to use his inside voice…I know, but I forgot…Yes, I read the plan…Yes, I know about the breathing and the counting and the whispering…"

That's when I whispered, "Fuck you," and hung up. I looked over at Dward and he flashed me a shit-eating grin while he rubbed his eye with his middle finger.

There's no such thing as the Least Restricted Environment in a public school. Ask any student from the brightest to the dullest; school is no place to send a kid…unless you want to break his spirit and squash his creativity.

For forty years one of my annual Freewrites had been
School is like _____.

And every year the sad sacks before me filled in the blank with JAIL! I asked them to support that outrageous claim, and year after year they were able to do so…easily.

"Too many dumb rules."

"Name one." I challenged.

"Lavatory passes. It's dumb that you need a pass to go to the lavatory."

"Another."

"You can't talk all day."

"You can't work with your friends."

"Yeah. You can't even *sit* with your friends."

"They have lock downs and search your lockers."

"The food sucks."

"The principal is like a warden."

"And what about us, your teachers?"

"Guards!"

"Anything else?"

"It's a 12-year sentence with no time off for good behavior."

See? Everybody's environment is restricted.

Funny how we want Dward to fit in and be like everyone else by treating him differently! The *experts* say he needs Word Banks. They say he needs fewer multiple-choice items and preferential seating. He needs extended time for all tests and assignments. And for statewide standardized tests, he needs to take as long as he wants to finish. We will leave all other kids behind waiting for him to catch up.

The whole mess is a good IDEA gone bad. And it's not all the government's fault. Teachers, too, like to make up obfuscatory acronyms. I'll bet that there's at least one department in every school that is secretive. At Facade Junior High where I got my start, it was the Reading Department. Theoretically I was its chairman, but practically I never knew what it was doing. It wasn't that I wasn't interested; I just didn't have the necessary security clearance.

'What are you doing this week, Mrs. Chaste?" She had the greatest legs in the school. Kids were always dropping pencils in her room.

"DRTA's."

"How about you, Mrs. Thrice?"

"USSR."

"SQ3R."

"SQRQCQ"

I tried the acronym route a few times myself. Of course it got me in trouble.

"Mr. Angelo, I caught one of your students in the hall with *SHIT* on her pass," said the nervous and humorless Assistant Principal.

"Well, she did say it was an emergency," I smiled.

"No, you don't understand, Mr. Angelo. The *word* SHIT was written on the pass...and it was signed by you. Here, look."

"Oh, I see. *You* don't understand. That's just an acronym...S.H.I.T. It stands for **S**tudent **H**elper **i**n **T**ransit." I kept smiling as he tried to absorb my reasoning.

Then more misunderstandings over the phone. "Mr. Angelo? This is the Attendance Office. You have *SHIT* on your attendance slip again this morning. You're going to have to stop this," said the matronly Mrs. Mendenhall, the Attendance Officer.

"I can't; I'm regular," I quipped.

"That's not funny, Mr. Angelo." She was always telling me that.

"That's an acronym, Mrs. Mendenhall. It stands for **S**pare **H**omerooms **I**nane **T**edium."

"That's not funny either." She hung up without laughing.

To save face before my class…who always stopped working when the phone buzzed—they don't ring in public schools, you know—I continued the conversation. "You know, Mrs. Mendenhall, my students were just talking about you…They said that you sure are their favorite attendance officer…Yes, they really did. (Boos could be heard in the background.) And they said to tell you that you really look pretty today. (Hisses now.) Yes, they really did…They want to know if you'd be embarrassed if they chartered the Mildred Mendenhall Fan Club?" (Chants of "Hang it up! Hang it up!")

"Mr. Angelo, I'm a bit upset with the unprofessionalism you exhibited in response to my memorandum of the 26th. The Anglo-Saxon expression was neither warranted nor appreciated. Would a simple *no* have been too much to ask?" The high school chair, my competition for the new Language Arts Supervisor position, was easily shocked and easily impressed by big words.

"You don't understand, Miss Shrapnel. My answer was *yes*. That was an acronym. It stands for **S**ubmit **H**onorably **i**n **T**ension." I don't think she believed it.

Although I was never very successful at it, all that acronymic code-talk allowed the Reading Specialists to get away with the proverbial murder. Nobody asked; they didn't tell…and not too many kids learned how to read.

"Harry has dyslexia."

"Poor home environment."

"Black."

"Puerto Rican."

"Stupid."

"Well, what can I do to help him in my class?"

"He needs to be tested."

"Could you do that tomorrow?"

"Not likely. Harry needs to have a complete battery to gauge his strengths and weaknesses."

"His weakness is that he can't read."

"You're too much, Tony. Did you hear that, Mrs. Thrice? Tony says Harry can't read. Ha, ha, ha, ha."

"Could I see his folder?"

"See his folder?! Oh this is too rich. He wants to see his folder. Tony, Tony, Tony. Reading folders do not leave the room. They never have; they never will. If you want to see one, you'll have to get administrative clearance. Imagine! See his folder! Ha, ha, ha, ha, ha."

"Let's go in and have some cake, Gar." That's what Italians do…we eat. When we're happy, we eat. When we're sad, we eat. When we meet a twenty-year-old kid who already knows what's wrong with public education, we eat. No matter the emotion, we eat.

So I'd get over this kid…over a full stomach.

YOUR PRINCIPAL IS YOUR PAL

What is wrong with public education? Just about everything. From the nation to the state to the local school board, the layers of bureaucracy and special interest groups stand ready to stifle and demoralize America's 2.1 million teachers. Not many of us last beyond five years. The dinosaurs that do either become curmudgeons or robots. I've been called the former and take it as a compliment. Principals have been called the latter…and, not surprisingly, they have taken it as a compliment as well.

I've never mastered the fine art of getting along with building principals, even after decades of trying. I used to worry about it, but now I don't give a shit.

Principals I have known have been insecure, dogmatic, insensitive, petty, and former phys ed teachers. They are so consumed with self-preservation that there is time for little else. They want to be principals forever.

One, especially, was a lodestone of mediocrity. He was always there when you didn't need him. Part of his strategy was to hound you from the time you entered **HIS** building to the time **HE** deigned you could leave. I didn't know if he was a saunterer or swaggerer. He walked like his boxers were stuck in his crack and he was too much of a gentleman to yank them out. He'd enter the Faculty Lounge at precisely 7:30 and simultaneously glance at the clock and your coffee-filled mouth. He'd cough in your direction, get red in the ear lobes, and try to separate his cheeks on the way out.

My first year of teaching when I sported a crew cut…flat on top…and an olive green suit with plaid lapels a la the Beatles, I was afraid of him. And I think he knew, just like a dog would know. He popped in and out of my room with nauseating regularity and never found anything right. The rows were crooked, the blinds were slanted, the bulletin boards were dull and the kids were loud. I was always sorry about everything and vowed to straighten up rows and blinds, jazz up bulletin boards, and shut up kids. That's what principals like, everything straight and everything quiet.

This guy had seven reasons why I should be teaching something else. He also had seven fingers. Maybe seven and a half. I couldn't be sure, and I didn't want to stare. He was the one who told me I should be teaching formal grammar to my slowest, dullest class. Back in the 60's they were called R-7's, average minus, and there were always more than forty of them. Today they are called Academic, all destined for *safety schools*. He told me it was my duty as their English teacher to drill them into submission. Not gutsy enough to resist, I relented.

The class in question wrote stuff like:

> He about 9 he got black curly Hair bpal tigth curls he. has a dark. complexion; and wear old dirty wholly shoes and black ugly you fgo villp and your find him and their anthes onp more he was ug…

> Two boys were shaming windows in Town. The paleace chasing them, but they got away. One person has a good a the boys
> They weight about 140 they had head rages around ther head. They had black leather jacit. One had a big head the other had a big nose. the one with the head was short and the other was caring him…

But this was the kind of thing they wanted us to do: draw one line under the subject and two lines under the verb. That's what it said in Warriner's and you didn't mess with Warriner back in the day. You also had to circle stuff and draw arrows and then for the *piece de resistance*, you had to diagram the works. It's still pretty much that way today only now the kids in the sentences you have to diagram are called Ja'meer, LaShonda, and Jesus. And they go to the *bodega*, not the store.

I didn't think these kids were ready for that kind of assault so I decided *we* would conjugate verbs, just the regular ones because they'd never believe that "brang" was not a word. On the first day *we* did the present, past and future tenses. They thought the whole thing was pretty ridiculous.

I walk	we walk
you walk	you walk…
he, she, it walks	they walk

"Why you do the same one twice?"
I ignored him.

Every kid…whether he wanted to or not…had a turn to conjugate and whenever he got to the third person singular, he rattled it off so fast it sounded like I, you, he shit! They thought that part was neat.

We continued this I-you-he-shitty lesson for one long excruciating week. Then I thought the class was ready for some kind of check up test. I passed out ditto sheets. They loved ditto sheets. Well, they loved the smell of ditto sheets, especially when they were warm off the drum. My R-7's snorted the toxic vapors of the fluid, pulled it into their lungs and smiled shit-eating grins.

The directions on the sheet were simple:
Conjugate the following:

1. walk

2. talk

3. start

Know what I got?

I the following
you the following
he shit the following

I learned two things that Friday: conjugating verbs was a dumb drill and my principal was a man with a paper asshole. You might be wondering…what's a paper asshole? I'm not exactly sure, but where I come from it's always applied to a guy who's a phony, who's full of shit, who doesn't know his ass from his elbow. The kind of guy Holden Caulfield could spot a mile away…and all.

"Have you been teaching grammar?" asked Paper A. out of the corner of his mouth.

"Yes," I lied out of the corner of mine. "And the kids really love it."

"I told you so," he said as he swaggered over to my windows and straightened the blinds. "English is grammar, you know."

"Oh, I know. I know."

What I did know was that my natural instincts and feelings about teaching should be more closely listened to and that Paper A. should be tolerated outside the sanctity of my classroom. It was the way you played the game...and Rule #1 was: Always launch into a grammar lesson when you're being observed.

If only this guy had a sense of humor. No such luck. I found that out one day when he stormed...his boxers were jammed way up there...when he *stormed* into the Faculty Lounge at 3:15, the end of my free period...make that *planning* period...a teacher is never allowed to be *free*...and the end of the school day. He had this mania about total teacher involvement, especially in the hallways. He wanted every teacher standing outside his door and in the hall to regulate the furious flow of student traffic and to keep out communist aggressors.

"Tony, how about coming out in the hall and giving us a hand?"

I got up quickly, went out in the hall, and clapped. Get it? Give us a hand? The only thing Paper A. got was red in the lobes. I stopped clapping and mumbled to the undulating mass of surly adolescents: "Okay. Let's keep moving. No shoving there. Don't stoop. Hey! Get your foot off his back..."

Caution: Faculty Meeting in Progress

Facade Junior High was a miniature representation of our community. I guess all schools are. It latched onto fads and movements and at the same time railed against them. The community was resistant to change of any kind. And so it spat its venom at the public school, which ironically hadn't changed in decades. Everything was the school's fault.

So it was.

So it is.

Back in the 60's the length of a kid's hair shadowed the length of the school day. An upturned collar, a skirt above the knee, open-toed shoes, jeans. These were the weighty issues that plagued the community, its parents, and its teachers. Noise in the halls took priority over *noise* in the classroom. Attendance records were given more attention than lesson plans.

> "Meetings. Don't we just love meetings? Every day, twice a day. We talk…I bet if I blew the conch this minute, they'd come running. Then we'd be, you know, very solemn, and someone would say we ought to build a jet, or a submarine, or a TV set. When the meeting was over they'd work for five minutes, than wander off or go hunting."

So said Ralph, one of William Golding's regressivists in *Lord of the Flies*. But he could very well be any teacher throughout these United States caught in the web of bullshit which is…drum roll here…**The Faculty Meeting**. Observe this from the hall so as not to be contaminated, but if you've had your shots…come on in:

The building principal, as articulate as the 43rd President of the United States of America, promptly calls the meeting to order. Speaking out of the corner of his mouth he congratulates his teachers for turning in interim reports on time. Back in the day these were five sheets of multi-colored paper with carbon backs that told parents…and everyone else in the district who got copies…that their kids were losers destined for quarterly failure. Nothing personal. Nothing positive. Nothing worthy of the refrigerator.

Although they all smile and nod, the teachers don't really pay attention to the proceedings. The art teacher sits at the far left, alternately tracing Gothic and Roman letters. She never looks up.

The English teachers grade their papers. They always grade their papers. Everywhere they grade their papers. Through lunch. During hall and cafeteria duties precariously balancing stacks of themes on uplifted knee, they grade.

The football coach and his assistants work on this week's plays and smile expansively because they get to leave early. They grade nothing. Nor do the Home Ec teachers. But they deftly clip coupons from the daily newspaper. Nowadays they call themselves Food and Consumer Scientists. How's that for bullshit? The Social Studies teachers complain about everything that smacks of freedom. Put to referendum they would defeat the Bill of Rights.

"Too many kids in the halls without official passes."

"Yeah. Some teachers are scribbling on any old scrap of paper."

"And they don't put the time on it."

"Or the destination."

Although the complaint seemed to be general in nature, it was directed towards me. The faculty knew that I hated the notion of passes, especially for lavatory use. They knew that I regularly scribbled my initials on anything handy and sent my students out into the Land of Oz. There they would quickly be accosted by hall monitors and be relentlessly interrogated under glaring florescent lights.

"Where are you going?"

"Lav."

"Where are you coming from?"

"Room 27." I always told the kids to say they were coming from room 27. My room was 112.

"Who's your teacher?"

"Mr. Rangelo."
"Figures."

The Overture begins with hall-procedures, gum-chewing policies, study hall conduct, athletic eligibility rules, and room arrangements. There is much ado about nothing, but the sound and the fury of it go on for 60 minutes. That which would be construed as utter nonsense in the classroom is transformed into acknowledged wisdom in **The Faculty Meeting**. The teachers question and misunderstand the obvious.

"Mr. Paper A., do I have this right? We're supposed to take roll at the beginning of every period?"
"Yes, it's the only way we're going to nip baggers in the bud."
"And we're supposed to check the master absentee list to see if kids who are present but marked absent are reported as present and vice versa?"
"Yes. In this way we will have complete accountability."
"And we're supposed to check the master list against the music department list?"
"Yes indeed. Kids taking instrumental lessons are not to be marked absent."
"And we're supposed to check these lists against those put out by the guidance department and the athletic director?"
"Yes."
"I can't do it."
"What?"
"I don't have a hook on my door."
A chorus of room-wants goes up. Someone begs for a pencil sharpener.
"After all, Mr. A., mine's been broken since last Christmas."
"Wanna screw for it?" puns the Faculty Fool.
"I've been requisitioning staples for over two months but all I keep getting is staplers. I now have five but not one staple."
"That's nothing. I ordered 3 packs of 5 by 7's. Know what I got? Seven packs of 3 by 5's. What am I going to do with 7 packs of 3 by 5's?"
"Want to swap? I'll give you one stapler and take the 3 by 5's off your hands for a box of staples."
Then the thrill of the open market fills the room. Wheeler-dealers grab the moment to outbid each other. Ruinous bargains are made. Old friends are lost.
"Okay but don't take the filing cabinet out of my room until you put that hook on my door!"

"Wanna screw for it?"

See? What I had hoped was going to be a teacher's valid complaint about valuable class time wasted on roll-taking turned out to be the beginnings of another wasted faculty meeting.

Paper A. restored order and proceeded. "The Assistant Paper A. (What? You thought one guy could screw it up all by himself?) will now explain procedures to be followed for the taking of student pictures." (He said *pitchers.*)

"Thank you, Mr. A. As you all know (They always told us stuff that we all knew.) Statewide Pictures will be here tomorrow to take pictures."

"Will they bring 'em back?" Faculty Fool was on a roll.

"Good one, F.," smiled Asst. P.A. who always showed too much teeth when amused. "Now to make things run smoothly and to cause as little inconvenience (*to the photographer*) as possible, I'm asking that you follow these procedures. First, at 8:01 students whose last names begin with the letters A to F are to be excused from their English classes, on the first floor only, to report to the stage of the auditorium. They are to form two lines, one for kids who want to buy their pictures and one for kids who don't. English teachers are to accompany these students to the auditorium. At 8:01 all teachers who are free at this time are to cover the English classroom. Of course, that's on the first floor only." Another smile. More teeth. "Now, at 8:11 the English teachers will return with the A to F's and pick up the G to L's and go back to the auditorium."

"Question!"

"Yes?"

"What if you only have one kid in the A to F category? Should we hold him for the 8:11 G to L's?"

"Good question. *(Yeah, so's Who's Afraid of Virginia Wolf?)* I would say keep to the schedule as outlined. If we make one change, then someone else will claim he has no G to L's and would want to sneak his M to R's in earlier than planned. And you know what would happen then." *(Paradise Lost, no doubt.)*

"Why is it always the English Department?" I asked, righteously indignant. "We get stuck with yearbook orders, guidance surveys, minority head counts, aptitude tests…and what's going to happen to our classes tomorrow? Why couldn't an entire class have their pictures taken instead of all this A to F shit?"

This caused Polly Purim to wince. No big deal since Polly winced at smokers, cursers, and misusers of the English language. She was a debit to my department…but more about her later.

"Good question, Tony. We'll take that into consideration for next year."

Normally I would have pursued the matter further, but it was already 4 o'clock and a number of my colleagues were growing restless, mumbling things like "I have a hairdresser's appointment for 4:30."

"Who do you go to?"

"Mr. Michael. And you know how *he* gets when you're late."

Paper A. then called on the head of the Guidance Department who told us how swamped she was with course selection business. She had this annoying habit of punctuating all her sentences with oh's.

"I'm sure you all know that course selection is upon us. Oh! And we want to make things run smoothly and cause as little inconvenience as possible. Oh! *(Sound familiar?)* We in the Guidance Department are asking that you follow these procedures. Oh! On Monday English teachers will be explaining to their students their recommendations regarding tenth grade English. Oh! All other subject teachers will be doing the same. And at the end of the day all sheets are to be returned to the English teachers who will count and alphabetize them and then turn them into the Guidance Department."

"Oh," I said, "shit!"

Ol' Polly winced again.

More from Paper A. "This is the time to tighten up the ship." This bit of nautical nausea always heralded the spring season. "We've got to clamp down now that the weather has improved and kids want to be out. We've got to be more *dilgent* on hall duty." Whenever you thought he mispronounced a word but you weren't sure, you just had to wait a minute because he'd do it again. "We've got to *dilgently* check those passes. Be sure kids are where they're supposed to be. Don't be afraid of confrontations. If we don't do this, who will do this?"

Could you believe it?

At 4:10 we'd finally got to the good stuff...the Chairwomen of the Hearts and Flowers and Coffee Fund Committees. Hearts and Flowers reported that although we were still in the black, we had only $15 left in our account.

"So I'm afraid that we're going to have to institute some changes. First, a teacher who is out sick a week will receive only a Get-Well card." A few oh's from the faculty. "I'm sorry but a teacher'll have to be out at least two weeks to qualify for flowers. Second, in order to cut down on babies, only a teacher who has worked here for at least three years is eligible for the Sterling Silver Spoon Set *for the first child only*. Second and succeeding issue, regardless of tenure, will receive the standard Congratulations on Your New Arrival card. Third, we were forced to redefine Death in the Immediate Family. In-laws are out." Lots of oh's this time. "I'm sorry but in order to cut down on deaths, a teacher is entitled to a carnation spray or chrysanthemum basket, depending on the season, for himself—God forbid—his wife, and his children, up to three. In-laws will now be in the With Deepest Sympathy card category."

"Thank you, Hearts. Coffee?"

"Well, things aren't much better in the coffee department. And I guess we all know why. Some of us are not paying our fair share. And you know the price of coffee and sugar these days. I have made a list of all teachers and beginning with the next pay, everyone will be assessed $1. That will be $2 a month."

"I don't drink coffee in the Lounge," asserted Mrs. Purim. "There's entirely too much smoke down there and my condition won't permit it. Why can't there be a coffee pot on the second floor?"

"No," said Paper A. quickly. "We can't have that. I said many times before that two coffee pots would split the faculty up into cliques. I want one unified staff and one pot is the only way to get it."

Samuel Sullen, another dissatisfied customer, struck a blow for tea drinkers. "Why should I have to pay two dollars a month for hot water?"

"And don't forget about all the smoke, Sam," coughed Polly.

Paper A., in an unusual gesture of compromise, said, "Good point, Sam. What we'll do is assess tea drinkers 50 cents a pay. All in favor say aye." Democratic pause.

"The ayes have it."

"That's still not right," said Sam quietly to Mrs. Purim.

"And what about all the smoke?" offered Polly. And then they both clucked and nodded.

"I know you're anxious to get outta here so unless anyone has anything for the good of the order, the meeting is adjourned," said Paper A.

Golding's Ralph was saved at the end. No such luck for America's teachers. Not even in 2004, an enlightened technological age. When I retired the faculty meeting was the same as when I began...only now it was all on PowerPoint.

She'd make a comment and then flip the book open to an excerpt that she read like a trained actress. I felt warm inside. I was falling in love…with her AND Milton.

She was the only teacher who ever gave me anything except a detention or a slap across the face. Scratch that *detention*. In my day there was no such thing. You were either hit or worked. I had thought that beatings were behind me when I was allowed to go public. I thought only Sisters of the Immaculate Heart of Mary were licensed to beat the shit out of me. When I met Mr. Willard, I learned how wrong I was. He was the shop teacher. He had polio when he was a teen and was left with a withered right leg that he lifted and swiveled as he walked. The all-boy class would mock him when he was late to class, which was often because he had a hard time getting up the steps. One day my new seventh grade friend Billy was shaking his leg in imitation of Mr. Willard. He'd swivel up to the black-board and tell us to get out our pencils for mechanical drawing. That's all we ever did. Draw. We never touched a piece of wood the whole year. Let me amend that. *Some* of us never touched a board. *Billy* was not so lucky.

Billy was writing on the board while we laughed at his apt performance. When we stopped, he turned around…and saw Mr. Willard standing in the doorway. Like Queen Victoria, he was not amused. He told Billy to go over to the wood-pile and select a board. Billy knew what was coming so he selected a 6-inch sliver of cast off plywood. Mr. Willard took it, placed it behind his ear as though it were a mechanical pencil and proceeded to select a board of his own. Looked like a 2 X 4 from where I was sitting.

"Bend over, Billy. And grab hold of your ankles." We all heard the swoosh and slam and cringed for Billy.

Mr. Willard would make a great nun.

But the only thing Dr. Jergen *hit* me with was a book she presented to me one Christmas. It was *Teaching As A Subversive Activity*. She told me to memorize Chapter 5. It was entitled "On Being a Crap Detector." She was convinced my writing was full of it and this chapter would teach me how to flush. I'm ashamed to admit that I wrote stuff like: In promulgating your esoteric cogitations, beware of platitudinous ponderosities.

She wrote stuff like: F/F…See back for comments.

And back there she'd write something like: "Christ spoke simply. Why can't you?"

How could you not like her? She was brilliant. She was funny. She was kind. And I wanted to be just like her. I took everything she taught even managing to get a B in one course. I went back to my classes and saw my students differently...which caused me to treat them differently. I always liked them, but now I loved them. And I loved what I was teaching. I even started to love grading papers. Well, *LIKE* them anyway.

I never told Dr. Jergen that she was my idol. I tried to. One day I had my students write a school memory from their elementary days. Dr. Jergen came to mind so I wrote about her. The kids shared and so did I. One smart ass raised her hand and asked if I ever told her how I felt. When I said "NO" they booed me.

On the way home that day I took a detour to my long ago graduate school. I went to the English office and asked to see Dr. Jergen. "I'm sorry," said the secretary, "but Dr. Jergen passed away two years ago."

I was a sad Humperdink all the way home. But there was not a teaching day that went by that I didn't think of her, act like her, talk like her. She was a *REAL* teacher and she deserved more than the summers off. I just wished I could have told her.

THE BLIND LEADING THE HALT

I continued to crank out six-page editions of my local union's propaganda news-letter. Piece after piece was inspired by the layers of bureaucracy that like the poor will always be with us.

And I continued to suffer the slings and arrows of negative feedback. But I didn't let any of that bother me. In fact I turned the ol' frown upside down. I was a channel of peace bringing light and wisdom not only to my fellow teachers but also to my first period class as I shared with them the wonders of the well-crafted sentence.

But I was stumped ten minutes into the period. I mean, what do you do with a seventeen year old freshman who, when told to write three sentences in which the subject of each sentence is a series of three or more common nouns, writes:

I for information, center, an answer telephone, fling an fix telephone.
I had a job for 3 mounts December, October, July,.
I teach music I even give sing less an I give drummless.

What if you told him to write three sentences each of which contains a series of three or more adjectives? And what if he writes:

I went to be Business men and a index card men
I went to be a Bank teller and durn pike teller an telephone teller
I work in Bank Store an Factories

I know what you do. You don't assign such shit for writing topics, that's what. Know how I found that out? Big Harry, one of the 'older' boys in the class, told me.

"Yes, Big Harry?"

"Mr. Rangelo." Big Harry and the others in the class could never quite get my name right. "Mr. Rangelo, I ain't writin' this shit. It don't make no sense."

"It *doesn't* make *any* sense, Big Harry."

"Solid on that," said Big Harry, oblivious to the correction.

"What would you like to write about?" I was accounting for individual differences. Nowadays I'd be dipping into multiple intelligences.

"A pome," said Big Harry, rolling something he picked from his nose.

"Okay, do it."

"Solid on that," said Big Harry.

"How about you, David? What would you like to write about?"

"Dave's got big teeth," volunteered an anonymous voice in the back row.

"Yeah, he got big teeth like a wolf. He wanted for biting is own mutha."

"Say what, nigger?!" David was annoyed.

I gave David the look, the Teacher Look. You know the one. It usually worked.

"My bad. Sorry"

"He still a wolf man."

"And you a mutha!"

"Alright, alright let's keep everybody's mother out of this," I refereed. "We've had an interesting discussion, now let's get to our writing."

"Rangelo got a big nose." I let that one go…partly because I was having a good day and partly because I do have a big nose.

David the Wolfman, decided to write a 'friendly' letter to Uncle Baron, a character in the novel *The Nitty Gritty*. Uncle Baron cheats his young nephew out of some money, involving him in a cock-fighting scheme which backfires. The ending…the uncle leaves the nephew stranded and broke…infuriated David.

Read his letter:

Dear Uncle Barnon

What's happing creep. You know you made off with my motherfucken cash and I didn't, even catch your ass but your ass is grass so you better stay away bitch you fucken faget. When I catch you I'll cut you too short to shit and dare you to bleed bitch

Your's Truly,

Meanwhile, Big Harry was madly at work on his 'pome.'

Misty moriining clouds in the sky with a worneng
A wizard walks by. Duck'd in his shadow's weving his
spill. With all the people wtinkil lk twinklngng Bell's.
Never talking, Just keep's walking He up with His
magic
What's this that stands Before me, A
Figuer in Black that points at me, turn around quick and
Start to run, findout that you're the chosen one. oh no no
please god help me. Is it the end my friend? sation's
the people Better goand beware
No no please
No.
        Not doun

"Can I go to the can?"
"He went in homeroom, Mr. Rangelo," squeaked the anonymous voice.
"That right, Big Harry?" I asked, turning away from Phyliss the Booper. (So named because her trademark was making noises that sounded like BOOP-BOOP. I asked her why she booped and she answered, gyrating like a seasoned Revivalist, "Mr. Rangelo, when I feel it, I do it. BOOP!")
"I got the runs."
"Can I go after him? Boop!"
"Can't you wait until the end of the period, Phyliss?"
"She missed her period." More from the anonymous voice.
"And you gone be missin' your big buck teeth, boy," countered Phyliss.

"I'm after Phyliss."

"You after anything, you ugly sex fiend!"

"You didn't let me go Friday so I should get to go now."

"Okay, okay," I interrupted. "Big Harry goes first...then David, then Phyliss, Donna, Hampton, Cyclops (so named because he had one eye bigger than the other) then Comet and Cupid and Donder and..."

"You jive, Mr. Rangelo," said Big Harry as he gracefully scooped up the wooden lavatory paddle and strolled out the room.

A few minutes later, Big Harry was back. He had the principal with him.

"Mr. Angelo, does Harold belong in your class?"

"Yes, Mr. P.A. Har..."

"Well, what was he doing in the lavatory?" asked Paper A. dangerously.

"Takin' a shit." That same anonymous voice.

"Who said that?" demanded the Paper Asshole. "Alright, get this. No one is to leave this class for any reason during the first period. Don't you *ladies* and *gentlemen* have toilets at home?"

"David don't," offered Cyclops.

"Anybody with a big ol' eye best shut his big ol' mouth." This was obviously one of David's sensitive days.

"Thank you for returning Big Harry, Mr. P.A. You can rest assured that we have more important things to do than make unnecessary trips to the lavatory. In fact, we were just in the middle of conjugating some irregular verbs..."

"Big Harry irregular."

The bell rang and the class stomped and booped its way out.

"Later, Ranj."

"Later, Big Harry."

"You got hairy arms, Mr. Rangelo."

"Thank you, Donna."

With the second period came a complete transformation. These were the *smart* kids. They hurried into the room, not daring to be caught in the hall before the warning bell sounded. They quickly sat, opened their notebooks, and waited politely for my professorial profundities.

"Does anyone have to go to the lavatory?" I asked. Of course no one did. Smart kids never have to go to the lavatory.

One of the many rules at Facade Junior High was that teachers must report to the main office between periods to check their mailboxes for important messages. It was always a wasted trip unless it was alternate Wednesdays—payday—so I generally skipped a period here and there. But since I already had one visit from

"I just wish his face wasn't so mean looking. I like English and all and I realize it's an important subject but..." Millicent's voice trailed off and her eyes misted up.

"Do I scare you, Millicent?" asked A.P.A.

"Oh no!" she said quickly. "You have a nice face...a kind face. Both of you do. (Let the record show that she was looking at the counselor.) See his hairline? (Now she was looking at me.) How it recedes on both sides? That's the mark of evilness. And his eyes are too dark. They penetrate...that's a bad sign."

"You're right; they *are* dark. I never noticed before. Don't you think they're dark, Mr. Wright?" consulted A.P.A.

"Yes, they're dark all right," concurred the counselor.

"Well, Millicent, we're certainly glad you called all this to our attention. Aren't we, Mr. Angelo? Now that we all know what the problem is, I'm sure Mr. Angelo will make every effort to do something about it. Won't you, Mr. Angelo?"

"Yes, Assistant P.A. I certainly will," said I with undisguised sarcasm.

"Fine. Now, Millicent, why don't you return to class and try to have a good day."

"Isn't she a nice young lady?" said the counselor.

"Sure is. We could use a lot more like her," said A.P.A.

"We could use a lot less of the bullshit you two twerps dish out," I said angrily. "I gave up my free period to sit here and listen to two horses' asses and a teenage twit discuss my evil eyes and faulty diction." My voice was rising steadily. "Both of you are about as competent in education as spastics are at a quilting bee."

"Let's not malign the unfortunate, Mr. Angelo. That's where Group can help you," said the counselor.

"I don't want to be *helped*, Wright! At least not by you! You two are like the blind and the halt..."

"There you go again, Mr. Angelo. The blind have their place in society, too," said the counselor.

"He's right, Mr. Angelo. But what's that *halt* part all about?" asked A.P.A.

"Another slur on the handicapped. Now in Group that would have been picked right up. He would have been forced to see that these remarks are only outward signs of his deep-seated feelings of fear and hostility generated by those less fortunate. Bad sign, Mr. Angelo...shows lack of confidence. Do you often feel threatened?"

"Wright, I have more confidence in my *gonads*—that's in the health text too—than you have in your entire Group! I really don't believe this conversation.

I really don't. What the hell do you want me to do—have plastic surgery...eye transplants...hair weaves?"

"You forgot about the a's at the end of your words," added the Assistant Paper Asshole.

"That young lady will have to get *used* to my voice, my face, my hair, my eyes, my everything! And she'll have to do it *every* day...*in my class*, not in your Group. I am not an ogre. I do not have satanic eyes, dark as they may be. I do not eat little children. I am a sympathetic and sensible adult who really likes kids. And you can ram your Group up your hairless ass. And *you*, well...you're just a shame!" And with that I rose and waded through the ankle high shit on the floor. As I was going through the door I heard "...another example of hostility. If it continues to go unchecked..."

"I thtill don't get that 'halt' part."

I closed the door and marched my ugly self down the three flights of stairs muttering "Boop, boop, boop, boop..."

PALOR GAMES

Maybe the counselor was right. Maybe I *was* insensitive.

Prejudiced teachers who discriminate against the kids seated before them are lethal. Their unthinking remarks, their insults and jabs, and their sarcasm all grow into cancerous tumors as their tenure wears on. Minority kids, usually black ones, bore the brunt of brickbats back in the sixties.

People who meant well wanted to call attention to the problems of racism by getting in touch with their inner selves. Usually this meant public confession in a room full of strangers with *mea culpas* going around a circle of penitents as tears were shed and group hugs were shared. I was curious so I went to one. They were called *sessions* back then. My wife called them *cults*. She saw no reason for me to go. She thought it was a lame excuse to get out of the house for a night away from our kids. I feigned shock and invited her to come along to shake off the shackles of discrimination and to get in touch with her feelings. She declined in a most profane way, so I went alone.

The lady in charge was part Negro and part Indian. (Terms like African-American and Native American were yet to be invented. 'Black' was used but never in mixed company.) She was a recognized leader in the Negro community, even though she was the only black face in her entire township of lily-white liberals. She welcomed us to her *studio*. I had never been in a *studio* before. Where I come from you had a *palor*. Then you had a dining room…that you only used at Christmas…then a kitchen and then a back room, which, you'll remember, was really another kitchen. There was no *studio*. Only the photographer had a studio…and you only went there when you got married.

I took in the surroundings. There were white tiles on the ceiling, wood panels on the wall. There was a piano in the corner so I assumed she had some cash. The chairs were draped in faded floral slipcovers. My mother could have told her that's what happens when you don't use plastic. There were lots of lit candles all over the place. I looked around for a statue of the Blessed Mother. Did I tell you I was Catholic?

The room was filling up with small talk and smoke. Everybody smoked in those days, liars more than others. The session was turned over to a skinny white woman named Mona who explained Dialogue Groups and what could be accomplished through them. She then went on to malign middle class values as she cast aspersions on two-car garages and Main Line Protestants. I had a one-car garage and it was unattached. Plus, as I said before, I was Catholic. For me climbing to the middle class was a lifetime achievement. But based on what Mona said, that was nothing to be proud of. She said we didn't have to agree with her; in fact, she insisted upon it. I admired her democratic spirit.

Not surprisingly Mona blamed her prejudices on her wickedly middle class parents. They had filled her young head with all kinds of negative notions about blacks. It was her mission, she said, to rise above their ignorance. Italian kids in my neighborhood would never badmouth their own parents like that. And we'd beat up anyone else who did. She was right though. About the negative notions, I mean. The pollacks were my family's scapegoats. They talked funny and smelled of cabbage. They cheated and they lied. We were told not to play with them. They went to their own school and church and we went to ours. We never prayed for them.

I never heard a bad word uttered about blacks other than my grandfather's calling them *ditzoons* and eggplants. None lived on my street but they would have been welcomed as improvements over all the Poles who lived in the next borough just steps away from my house.

When you take turns at speaking, what you generally do is practice what you are going to say instead of listening to what the other guy is saying. I was practicing my name while the guy next to me was baring his soul. He was a guidance counselor so he was good at it. "Man," I thought, "YOU are full of shit!" (Shit made up a large part of my vocabulary in those early years. Truth be told it's still way up there…with 'rat bastard.')

This counselor never talked to kids; rather, he *rapped* and *related to adolescents*. He never met a dumb kid; he just *encountered poorly motivated ones*. His office was open to all, he embraced everyone, and he understood everything. I felt like I was sitting next to the Statue of Liberty.

"My parents were upper middle class and I was brought up on the upper Main Line," he said as he lit a cigarette magnanimously bummed from the Negro militant to his right. That guy wore beads…a sign of militancy back then. So was his Afro and turtle neck sweater.

The counselor blew smoke in my face as he continued. "I went to an all-white high school. I never was much of a student but I managed to graduate and get into a state college." That pissed me off…then and now. I get sick and tired of those university snobs who badmouth state colleges, calling them safety schools, implying that even poor morons like me would be admitted. "I was what you might call a late bloomer," he said, all eyes riveted to his round, self-satisfied face. "I always wanted to do things with my hands…*yeah, like play with yourself,* I thought…build model airplanes, cars, stuff like that. I can still remember the smell of mucilage as I worked on the models. I get a real satisfaction out of seeing something grow under my hands, out of creating something from nothing," he continued.

"And the guidance counselor said 'Let there be model airplanes' and there were model airplanes and the counselor saw this was good," I thought as I lit my *own* cigarette.

The next one to share talked through his nose. He too admitted to being a late bloomer and to being a guidance counselor. The *studio* was crawling with counselors, a group that most teachers thought were in cahoots with administration. We envied everything about them. They were **REAL** professionals in that they could schedule their own day. They went to the bathroom whenever they wanted. They drank coffee at their desks while they worked. They had telephones and secretaries…and never went home with a briefcase full of papers to grade. They always blamed us for everything the kids didn't know.

"Don't you guys teach spelling anymore?"
"No. In fact we give extra credit for misspelled words."
"You should see their college application essays!"
"We don't teach writing either."
Come to think of it, *teachers* blamed each other for what the kids didn't know.

"Who said you could begin a sentence with a conjunction?"
"Mr. Angelo."
"Who said you should write the way you talk?"
"Mr. Angelo."

"It figures. Now I have to spend the rest of the year unteaching all that nonsense so you can get into a decent college." I only know this because kids would come back and tell me. They loved doing that.

"Well," I would say to the kids, "you just tell Mrs. So and So that I admire her professionalism and will do all I can to emulate her high standards."

"For real?"

"No way." And then we'd high-five each other.

The nasal counselor was droning on about fatherless boys. He knew what they felt because his own father had died two years ago. Two years ago? Shit! Mine died twenty years ago…when I was five. Here's what a kid feels when his father dies…anger…anger reaching rage. He's angry with his father, angry with his friends who have fathers, and angry with his God. He's angry with his teachers every June who insist that he make cards and gifts for Father's Day. He cries in his pillow at night. He punches the wall. He feels hurt every day until he finds someone to take his father's place. That's what a teacher can do…take his place. Not forever. Just 48 minutes a day, the time that the kid is in your classroom. I think that's why I wanted to be a teacher, but I wasn't going to share that with this crowd. My interpretation of *in loco parentis* was much too personal and private. In addition to being fatherless, when I was a kid I was very fat and very feckless. And I wasn't going to share that either.

Nasal said that like his fellow counselors he could *relate* to students. He liked to *rap* with them, *get down* with them on their home *turf*. This language game seemed to be the propensity of male counselors. It just got worse as the years flew by. When I left Facade after 40 years they were greeting their advisees with "Tzup? How's it hangin', my li'l bro? B'ave ya self, ite?" Now *that's* a safety school graduate, nigh mean?

Frances was next. She taught math in my school. She was what you'd call *handsome* today. She was also what you'd call *Tameek'qua* or *Quanteesha* today. But back then she was just plain ol' Frances. She never looked you right in the eye when she talked so you never knew if she was talking to you or the guy next to you. It wasn't her fault; it was just that one eye went one way, and one went the other way. She must have driven her students nuts.

She was fascinating to listen to though. She had experience after experience from her youth and beyond that shocked and inspired me. As she talked to the *Reader's Digest* condensed books that lined the studio walls, we learned that she was the only black in her neighborhood, that when she was a kid, she was the only black in her class, and that when she went to high school she was the only

"No, I'm a Negro…and it's Mary *ANN*."

I came to her rescue. Not Mary 'Jane's' but the teacher's. "C'mon, Miz Mary. Lez me and you be gone to da palor. Dey ain't got no watermelon in he-ah."

Dr. Mudd was eloquent and he was rich. When the neighbors found out he lived in the foxhunting country in one of those huge redwood contemporaries, they decided Mudd was the man for the job. To make it easier on their Republican consciences, he cross-filed. And, wonder of wonder, he was elected. Narrowly of course, but elected nevertheless.

"Now what, Dr. King?" asked my sarcastic wife. "You've got that look again."

"Alfie. We need to do something about Alfie."

Let me fill you in. Alfie was the black Assistant Superintendent of the Facade Area School District. He was convinced that the Director of Elementary Education was trying to kill him. He was convinced that his phones were being tapped. He was convinced that he was being set up for blackmail and resignation. And I was convinced that he was nuts.

Alfie wasn't his real name. It was a code name he selected during the height of his paranoia. He said that if I ever wanted to call him, I should ask for *Alfie* and then hang up. Then he would call me back on a secure phone.

Lots of rumors swirled around this guy. The teachers didn't have a clue what he did on a daily basis. He never visited our school, he never chaired meetings, and he never made public speeches. The whites among us were convinced his was a token position. He didn't have to DO anything. Just holding the second highest job in the district was good enough. It was affirmative action that caused negative reaction.

"He's screwing his secretary." That was the word in the faculty rooms around the district. "And she's married. Wait till her husband finds out." In fact her husband did find out and went to Alfie's office one day and punched him in the mouth. Alfie fell down, banging his head on his desk. The story that was put out to the press was that the Assistant had suffered a mild stroke and his workload would be cut in half while he recovered.

"I have the toxicological reports to prove it. He poisoned my Wheat Thins. He wants me out of there!" That's what Alfie told me.

"Tell the cops," I said.

"They're in on it."

"Tell the Superintendent."

"Him too. You're my only hope. They see you as a threat."

"Me? A threat? What can I do?"

"Your articles and your speeches. They know you know."

"Know what?"

"That they aren't doing their job. That they're selling the black kids short. That they're misusing federal funds."

My articles? I was impressed. I didn't think anyone actually read my articles. But I was usually careful in them, never mentioning names, just titles. Like this one:

GOING THRU CHANNELS

TEACHER: I've got this great idea about how to improve a student's reading ability at almost no extra cost to the district.

DEPARTMENT CHAIR: Sounds good to me but you know I'm not the last word.

TEACHER: I got this great idea about a reading program.

LANGUAGE ARTS SUPERVISOR: Does the principal know about this?

TEACHER: About this idea I have…

PRINCIPAL: Shouldn't you be talking to the Reading Coordinator?

TEACHER: In order to get the students to be better readers…

READING COORDINATOR: Isn't this in the area of elementary education?

TEACHER: Reading instruction could be improved by…

DIRECTOR OF ELEMENTARY EDUCATION: The ramifications go well beyond the elementary school…

TEACHER: My idea is…

DIRECTOR OF SECONDAY EDUCATION: Well, I'm in a bind. I have to cut budgets and all. Not much left for summer workshops. Now when I was principal, things were different. Anyway there's not much money. However, your idea is a good one. Of course, it does need more input but let me reiterate…

TEACHER: About this reading program…

ASSISTANT SUPERINTENDENT: Sh! Nobody knows I'm here!

TEACHER: A couple of years ago I had this idea…

SUPERINTENDENT OF SCHOOLS: This is fantastic. Share it with the School Board.

TEACHER: I appreciate the opportunity to share with you my idea for reading improvement…

SCHOOL BOARD PRESIDENT: You have three minutes for your comments, and yours are up. In the future, don't bother me, go through channels.

That's how it worked at Facade. And over the forty years I worked there not much changed…except the names of the guilty. The administrators went from one district to another like whores on call. This was the place where stuff trickled down, not where it bubbled up…where Gerard Manley, the repulsively fat School Board President, ruled with a big stick.

Teachers were not expected to attend school board meetings. If they did, their treatment was harsh and abrasive. Ol' Gerard, the chain-smoking despot, regularly reduced teachers to tears…right out there in public. He'd point his nicotine stained sausage finger at the *culprit* and tell her that she should be glad she had a job. He'd remind her that the poor taxpayers out there had to work hard for their money…and they had to do it eight hours a day…even in the summer.

Not many people attended the meetings back then. Just the army of toady administrators who sat in front and smiled and nodded. In Quaker County what brought the throngs of Republicans out were budget meetings. Gerard always gave them three minutes to rant and rave about the sheer waste of taxpayer money on things like new roofs, new books…you know, needless stuff like that. It was enough to make you chuck it all in for ballet…so you just didn't go. Instead you stayed home and marked your papers and planned your lessons and hoped for a better day tomorrow. Of course *I* went…every month…just so I could report back to the teachers via newsletter the abominations that transpired.

That Channel piece went over well with my colleagues. They stopped me in the halls and said stuff like:
"Read your article. Don't you have any essays to grade?"
"You never run out of things to complain about, do you?"
"Way to go, Tony. Where you workin' next year?"

But because Alfie was a reader, I thought I owed him something.

"You don't owe him *anything*," said my wife. "Keep your nose out of his business. It all sounds dirty…and dangerous."

She was right. She was almost always right. Alfie became Facade's Invisible Man. All his talk of things breaking, of the NAACP and the Human Relations Council storming Facade's administrative offices never materialized. He was all but forgotten…until the day he killed himself. There were no details in the local paper. Just one line…"He apparently died of a self-inflicted gunshot wound."

"This was not your fault so don't go moping around in the *palor* all day," said my wife. "Go out and get the mail."

The box was filled with the usual bills and junk and postcards…six of them…all unsigned:

> **You're just another liberal wop**
> **Cluttering up our educational shop.**
> **You're trying to make the school budget bigger**
> **To help another worthless nigger.**

I went to Alfie's viewing. It was my first experience with black funeral *palors*. Mine was the only white face in the packed room of elegantly dressed mourners. The place reeked of carnations and the noise level was reminiscent of my own family gatherings. Alfie's wife sat in the front row greeting the bereft with loud wails and an occasional recognizable phrase or two. "THEY KILLED HIM!" A white-gloved funeral director rushed over with a tissue and a glass of water. "They killed Dr. King too!"

People sitting behind her were nodding in agreement. "That's right," they said. "They always kill the good ones." They were slowly waving their arms in the air. "That's right, Sister. That's right." It was contagious, kind of like a holy wave. I resisted the urge to join in probably because I thought they were talking about me.

Alfie's wife rose and shuffled the five steps to her husband's coffin. "What am I going to do n-o-o-o-o-o-o-ow?" She screamed louder and longer than any of my aunts who played similarly dramatic *palor* games. She could really hold a note. I stayed just long enough to watch her faint.

I left feeling guilt, Catholic guilt, Catholic guilt that teaches: if shit happens, you deserved it.

Violence and Rejection

Some weeks nothing happens. Nothing bad, that is. You go to school. You teach your classes. You grade your papers. The principal leaves you alone. But I vividly remember this one week that was crowded with events. The first was the administrative directive ordering me to rip out the critical commentary in the back of 350 *Lord of the Flies* books. Some literary genius had suggested that the boys on the island weren't just killing sows; they were in effect raping their mothers.

I went immediately to the office and said, "Mr. Paper A., I'd like to discuss this directive with you."

"Good. I've had two phone calls (two is the magic number for administrators to panic) about that damn book from parents. (What syntax.) "These two broads were pissed off about all the violence and bloodshed in the book. And that rape stuff in the back. So if you just have your teachers tear out the notes, everything will be okay."

"The point of the book is law and order and what happens when there is none. The regression to savagery…"

"Tony, I don't want to hear another one of your lectures. Just rip out the notes."

"But the notes are merely one man's interpretation. And it's a rare kid who even bothers to read them," I protested.

"Just rip them out."

"But two parents shouldn't speak for eight teachers and 500 students. Two complaints in seven years is hardly justification for *Fahrenheit 451* tactics."

"How many tactics?"

"Never mind. I'll rip them out."

Enough of that. It was now time for fictional *Mice and Men*. I went back to my classroom to find Big Harry pretending to be Steinbeck's mentally challenged Lennie Small. "Oh that's soft," cooed Big Harry as he stroked classmate Donna's upper arm.

"He feelin' up Donna, Mr. Rangelo. Don't let him tend no rabbits."

"Alright, Big Harry, take a seat. It's not nice to molest Donna."

"That's okay, Mr. Rangelo," said Donna.

They often acted out the literature of the day, so I was careful never to choose stuff like *Lady Chatterley's Lover* or *Portnoy's Complaint*.

"We gonna finish that play?" asked David the Wolfman. He was referring to an adaptation of *To Kill A Mockingbird* I had written...at the Wolfman level.

"Well, I'm not sure you guys were paying much attention when we were reading," I said. It was a cheap trick plied on occasion for plot review.

"I was paying attention," shouted Phyliss. "Donna was pretending that she got raped by Big Harry. Boop!"

"Not quite, Phyliss. Donna was just reading Mayella Ewell's *part* and Big Harry was reading Tom Robinson's." I corrected.

"Big Harry's always woofin' on Donna. And she just take it like some kinda white trash," said Phyliss, obviously jealous of any attention Big Harry bestowed on the other young ladies.

"Now, Phyliss, those are exactly the kinds of statements we were talking about yesterday. What's the word, guys?" I asked.

"Prejudice!" They shouted.

"Yup! That girl's a prejudiced slut alright," said the anonymous voice in the back of the room.

"Who you callin' a slut?" said Phyliss turning around and eyeballing the entire congregation. "You got something to say to me you come and say it to my face!"

"You ain't *got* no face," said the anonymous voice.

Just then Mr. Paper A. showed up with his clipboard. That meant a formal observation...and a lesson in grammar. That's what English teachers do when they're being observed. Something safe. Math teachers send kids to the board to embarrass them with all the mistakes they made on last night's homework. Social Studies teachers pull down old maps and point to countries that no longer exist.

"Okay, class, let's pick up where we left off yesterday. Who can tell me the difference between a common noun and a proper noun?" I asked.

"What about the play?"

"We wanna finish that play."

"You said we was gonna read about the rape today, Mr. Rangelo. Jew forget?"

"Member that cardinal knowledge stuff we were talking about yesterday?" asked Big Harry.

"Okay, guys." They had me. So did Paper A. "The play it is! Cyclops, would you please pass out the booklets?"

They read and adlibbed after their frank fashion and enjoyed the hell out of themselves. Paper A. never cracked a smile; he just kept scribbling crap all over my evaluation sheet.

The second event of the week was the principal's *second* directive. *To Kill A Mockingbird* was no longer to be taught because it contained a rape scene.

I went immediately to his office and registered a formal protest. "Mr. Paper A., this book has been in our curriculum for five years. You yourself approved its inclusion. The School Board authorized the money."

"I didn't know there was a rape scene in it then," said Paper A. smugly.

"It didn't have a rape scene in it then and it doesn't have a rape scene in it now!" I shouted.

"Well, if you ripped it out, okay. Then you can teach it."

"But there is no rape scene. That's the point of the whole damn book. Nobody got raped. It's nothing more than the classic cry of Southern womanhood…"

"Not another lecture, Tony. I'm not in the mood. There's lots of other books these kids could be reading instead of all this violent stuff you keep throwing at them. Why just this last period you were telling the kids about carnal knowledge, for Christ's sake."

"That was yesterday," I corrected.

"I don't give a shit when it was. You got no business wasting valuable school time with *carnal knowledge*! And that damn play of yours was filled with profanity, for Christ's sake. That's all I need is for one of their parents to get a copy and come in here and ask me what the hell my teachers are teaching."

"Shit and damn…that's all. That's mild, isn't it?"

"Hell no!"

"Okay, I'll rip 'em out," I said as I left his office and returned to the sanctity of my classroom, *cardinal* knowledge in tact.

The next day yielded the principal's third directive. It simply said: SEE ME.
I was beside myself with individual attention.

"Shut the door behind you," said Paper A., obviously pissed off about something. "You did it again! Even after we had our little talk yesterday, you did it again!"

"What did I do?" I really didn't know.

"That story you wrote. I got phone calls about it. More violence. Jesus, Tony, what the hell are you trying to do to me...cut my throat?" He always accused me...and others...of violating bits and pieces of his anatomy. If we weren't cutting his throat we were sticking his head in a noose or biting his back or squeezing his nuts in a vise. "Every time my damn phone rings, it's about you."

"What did I *do*?"

"That story. The one about the kid dying in the alley. The one you gave to the long-term substitute."

"Oh, *that* story. He died in an apartment hallway," I corrected.

"What the hell's the difference?"

"It makes a lot of difference. You see, it was an assignment on artistic unity. What I did, I wrote the ending of a short story and asked..."

"I don't give a shit what you did. Why did you have to make it so violent?"

"Have you read it?"

"Of course I read it. Do you think I'd call you in here and ream you out about it if I didn't even read it? What do you take me for?" I swallowed hard. I hated it when he asked rhetorical questions but when he paused I figured he wanted an answer.

"I take you for a literary ignoramus. You know next to nothing about what I'm teaching and you care even less. Every time I try to explain something to you..."

"I don't need *you* to explain anything to *me*. I'm the **principal**, for Christ's sake. This is what I mean by your lack of professional judgment." He was referring to an unsatisfactory rating he had given me earlier in the year, one that was based on the content of my union newsletter articles.

"Don't start with that again. That unsatisfactory remark was removed from my record...if you'll remember."

"Yeah, well, that doesn't mean you can't get another one! And don't think I haven't been thinking about it! That and the recommendation for Language Arts Supervisor." Oh that sly blackmailing bastard!

"Alright. I'll rip 'em out."

Of course I didn't. There is not enough time in a day to rip out all the stuff some might consider offensive or in this case violent. The anthologies teachers are made to use are pitiful. They are the absolute worst. They were lousy 40 years ago; they are lousy today. Well, not so much lousy as *safe*. When it comes to violence, here's what the publishers say to writers and editors:

> Avoid any content that may be construed as violent or unsafe, including references to killing or being killed, bullying, weapons of all kinds (knives, guns, explosives, etc.) fighting, serious accidents or injuries (car or plane crashes), and discussion of death and dying. Avoid idioms that refer to these topics or that use the vocabulary around these topics in a figurative way. Exercise restraint in your references to battles, wars, tragedies, and disasters.

Sounds like all the things that make up the real world that teachers are so often accused of not being a part of. You don't find much of it in expensive, oversized, and heavy anthologies. What you do find is a Whitman's Sampler intent on total inclusion. That is, something written by a Mexican, a Russian, a Chinese, a South African, a Samoan Islander, a tortoise on the Archipelago. The key is diversity, not quality. And these diverse folks can't be engaged in conflict. But there's more:

> Avoid implying that families consist of a mother, father, and children.
> Single parents, grandparents, stepparents, stepsiblings, friends and neighbors can all make up a family.

Sounds like Sesame Street and that's great…up until the kids reach secondary school. That's when they start to see the rest of the world through those very friends and neighbors that surround them. That's when they start to ask questions, wonder about relationships, get in fights, encounter bullies, hear bad words.

One publishing company tells its writers to limit references to sweets and junk food. Instead, they are to show students eating healthful, balanced meals and nutritious snacks such as fruit. They offer these admonitions as well:

> Do not mention or show alcohol, use of drugs (including prescription and over-the-counter drugs), or smoking.

Oh and limit references to watching TV or playing video games.

I didn't know there were so many restrictions. I thought you wrote a book and mailed it away and then they sent you royalty checks. That's what I did anyway. I wrote a book and sent it to Doubleday, A Communication Corporation. They kept it for a long time before they sent it back. That and a letter. It began:

> Your manuscript was received by Doubleday and is being returned unread, for now. This letter explains why.
>
> The flow of manuscripts into the Doubleday editorial offices is so great that our readers are overwhelmed, and are therefore unable to give your worthy manuscripts the attention they deserve. We hope that you will understand the problem, and that we are still interested in "unsolicited" manuscripts.
>
> If you have a manuscript or a partial manuscript you wish Doubleday to consider, please follow these important steps:
>
> 1. Write us a letter describing your book. This will be read by an editor. If the editor is interested, you will be invited to send the manuscript. If not, you will receive a rejection letter.
>
> 2. Please do not send us a manuscript before you have had a reply to your letter. Such submissions will be returned.
>
> Incidentally, this is a procedure followed by many professional writers. It enables them to get a prompt response to their proposal, and saves them the time and expense of sending an entire manuscript to a publisher who might not be interested in it.

They signed it   Doubleday & Co. Inc.
                        Editorial Department

No Yours truly…no Sincerely…no anything.

I thought their letter deserved a response. So here's what I wrote back to them:

> Your rejection notice was received by Angelo and is being returned unread, for now. This letter explains why.
>
> The flow of rejection notices into the Angelo household is so great that my family is overwhelmed, and I am therefore unable to give worthy rejection notices the attention they deserve. I hope that you will understand the problem, and that I am still interested in "unsolicited" rejection notices.

If you have a rejection notice you wish me to consider, please follow these important steps:

1.   Write me a letter describing your rejection. This will be read by my wife. If she is interested, you will be invited to send the rejection. If not, you will receive a rejection letter.

2.   Please do not send me a rejection letter before you have heard from my wife. Such submissions will be returned.

Incidentally, this is a procedure followed by many married couples. It affords the wife an opportunity to become actively involved in the writing process and thereby renders her worthy of the book's dedication.

It must have gotten lost in the mail because they never wrote me back.

Ennui, Angst, and Malaise

Remember that Faculty Meeting I told you about? Where all the teachers were so mealy-mouthed and sycophantic? Well, lest you be discouraged, there is a place where teachers are courageous, where even the most timid is a match for Goliath. That place is the Faculty Lunch Room. It is here that teachers vent the venom of their spleens, casting the first of many stones at anyone who eats during a different lunch period.

"May I have that salad in the back, please?" I asked the cafeteria worker.
"There're all the same," said she caustically.
"Okay, then I'll take the one in the back," I said trying to be nice.
"What's so special about the one in the back?" she persisted.
"It doesn't have any hairs in it."
"Humph!" she said.

I sat down at an empty table so I could eat my hairless salad and mark my papers undisturbed. That's what I did most of my life, marked papers. Some years later when I had reached the silver anniversary of my teaching career, I was monitoring a study hall in the cafeteria. Some kid who obviously had no friends sat across from me at the front table. He watched as I read and marked up essay after essay. He wanted to know how I arrived at the 89% I wrote at the top of the paper.

"It's a good number, and I haven't used it in a while."

He asked me how long it took to read and grade each one. I told him.

"And how many years have you been doing this?"

"If I tell you, will you go away?" He said he would so I told him. "Twenty-five years."

At the end of the period he came up to me and said, "You have spent a total of four years grading papers."

"Thanks, kid. I needed to know that."

I was deep into reading a paper about *The Great Gilly Hopkins*. It's a novel about a fat kid and this paper was written by a fat kid. Both were sad enough to make you cry. "May I join you?" asked a sub.

"No," I said as she sat down opposite me and asked me to pass the salt. Funny how people can't believe a 'no' when they hear it. Funny too how they salt their food before they taste it.

Over at one of the other tables—the Jock Table—all the health and phys. ed teachers were discussing box scores, plays, horse races, and pools. It was *their* table and they always talked about the same things at it. If you wanted to talk about something else, you had to sit some place else. Like at the High Academic Standards Table. Here you would find good ol' Stosh Grabowski, the Faculty Pole. There wasn't anything he didn't know about Poland. Stuff like God created it first, Copernicus was the most important man in the whole world, kielbasa is for lovers, Cardinal Mindzenty lives, and a zloty saved is a zloty earned. Stuff like that.

He was something else at the beginning of every school year. He would carefully scrutinize the list of new faculty members looking for–ski's. And when he found some, he became a bold and boring barnacle.

"Hi there! Name's Grabowski. Stosh Grabowski. Welcome to Facade Junior High."

"Thank you. I'm Stella Kaminski."

"Kaminski? No fooling? Where are you from?" You could tell he was hoping for Warsaw.

"Doylestown."

"Oh," said Stosh forlornly and then brightened. "Doylestown. Our Lady of Czestochowa, right? That's where I got this miraculous medal and these rosary beads and…"

They used big words at the High Academic Standards table. Teachers who sat there were full of *ennui*. I only know because they often said so. I was content to think they were full of shit. Teaching to them was a stepping-stone. Don't ask me to what. Administration, I guess. Today they were feeling *angst*.

"I'd fail him…plain and simple," said Stosh. "Why should you curve a perfectly good test so that he could pass? They just want to be sure that he's eligible for baseball, that's all," he said lowering his voice and glancing over at the Jock Table. "By ninth grade he should know how to do a research paper and footnote it properly," he said now raising his voice and glancing over at My Table. Feeling *sangfroid*, I glanced back at him and rubbed my eye with my middle finger.

The Social Studies teachers had unsubstantiated opinions about everything. They were experts on the past, having taught the same drivel year after year. Nothing new was ever unearthed. They just cranked out textbook fact after textbook fact. Kids often complained about the ennui they felt on a daily basis. I told them to offer it up. Not even the Catholic kids knew what I was talking about. The world was changing. But the Social Studies teachers were unaware of it. What'd you expect? Stosh was the Chairman of the Social Studies Department.

He was always trying to recruit members from other departments to sit with all the smart guys at his table. He'd do a background check.

"Where'd you go to high school?" he'd ask the prospective new diner. If you heard Stosh say "oh…there," you knew the poor soul had to sit elsewhere. College matriculation was high on the list of Table Prerequisites. If it were a state school, you were deemed unworthy. If the tuition were laughably low, you were deemed unworthy. And ironically, if you majored in education, you were deemed unworthy. I hit the trifecta.

A teacher from my department passed all the tests. His credentials were impeccable. So was his pronunciation. He said both n's in annuity and the d in grandmother. Worthy of a seat at Stosh's right hand.

"I told him," intoned Stosh, "that he should get out of my class. I said 'Sam, you're never going to amount to anything. You are going to spend your life riding the back of a garbage truck,' I said." It was Stosh's basic premise that a human being could not reach adulthood nor could he become a contributing member of society unless he knew how some ancient Egyptians mummified other ancient Egyptians. "I said, 'Sam, do you know who Akhnaton is?' And he said, 'I thought current events day was tomorrow.'" And everyone at the High Academic Standards Table laughed uproariously.

"Would you please pass the pepper?" asked the sub.
"No," I answered.

one offered us suggestions. No one showed us HOW to do it differently. Some were too afraid to ask for help. Some were too indifferent. And some were too *perfect*.

One Paper Asshole—as you can see, that's what I call **all** principals—said to me once, "Come on now, Tony, you know as well as I that there are some lousy teachers in this school. You know who they are…I know who they are…even the kids know who they are."

"Well then," said I, "why do you rate them Satisfactory every year? Why don't you get rid of them?"

"Yeah right. I guess the union would let me do that."

Always the response. Blame the union. How dare the teachers to expect their union to protect and defend them. The union as the bad guy is easily sold to growing numbers of non-union workers out there in America. I guess you just have to be born into stuff to understand. I understand because I was born Italian, Catholic, Democrat, and Union. In Quaker County where I live the last two brand you as loser, lout, and locust…of the biblical variety. You know—a Plague on the populous swarming every three or four years during contract negotiations picking the pockets of senior citizens on fixed incomes.

I just threw that in to clear things up before you got too far and started thinking I was Anglo-Saxon, Presbyterian, Republican and Management.

There was always lots of room at My Table, probably because I used to tell off people in alphabetical order. I didn't waste time with 'I should have said;' I said it. But nobody *likes* you when you scratch where it itches. I never realized that until my brutally realistic wife asked me the heart-stabbing question. "Tony, do you have any friends?"

"What do you mean?"

"I mean, do you have any friends?"

"Of course I do. I have lots of friends."

"Name one."

"Karl."

"Name another one." See? She's brutal.

I thought for a second…and then for a minute. I couldn't come up with another name so I said, "A friend is like a home. If you have two of them, you don't really have any." That didn't even make sense to me, but when you're backed into a friendless corner you get desperate.

Only one friend. Pretty depressing, huh? And that one friend used to get me into most of my messes. Karl was the President of my local union and the guy who fed me all the hot poop for my newsletter articles.

"Hi, Karl, MY FRIEND," I said unnecessarily loud as I saw him heading toward My Table.

"Hi, Tony. Are you subbing for Miss Joness?" he asked my tablemate. (It should be noted here that *Joness* is not a misspelling. Just like some Smiths like to pass themselves off as Smythes, this toothless math teacher liked to pass herself off as Jone-ESS. And maybe she wasn't toothless but whenever I was stuck eating lunch with her, I never saw any. Oh, and all she ever ate were tuna fish sand-wiches. She just kind of broke them apart and gummed them into submission. (Jone-ess. She could have been Facade's mascot!)

"Yes."

"Well, your class just threw a set of Algebra I books out the third floor win-dow," said Karl.

"Oh gee," she said as she ran off without excusing herself.

"Dumb ass broad," said Karl. "Subs believe anything you tell 'em."

He slid my ungraded papers aside and gripped my arm. "Listen, this stuff you've been hearing about transfers…it's true."

"How do you know?"

"I'm being transferred; that's how I know!"

"You? To what?"

"Are you ready? English. Your department. How does that grab you?"

"How can they transfer a social studies teacher into English?"

"Just like that," he said snapping his fingers. "I have dual certification." He made it sound like a venereal disease.

"I didn't know you ever taught English."

"I never did. I got 18 lousy credits in undergraduate school and the bastards in Harrisburg gave me a minor in English. And that was over twenty years ago."

"Did you get official notification? I mean, maybe it's just another rumor." It should be noted here that schools are run on rumors. Rumors R Us! The only thing teachers spread more than bullshit is rumors.

"No," said Karl, "it's no rumor. It's coming. You can bet on it. What we should do is jump the gun on them."

"You mean a newsletter article?"

"Yeah. Something that makes them look stupid. You know?"

"Yeah, I know. But I'm getting tired of all the negative feedback."

"Tony, the teachers who say you're negative aren't worth your concern. Just forget about them. Now about this new article…"

And so My Friend at My Table conned me into still more propagandistic prose. The lunchroom, where the action is, gave birth not only to indigestion but to:

THE SCHOOLHOUSE SHUFFLE

Don't be misled; this is not a piece about the latest dance craze, nor is it about a new way to cut old cards. It's simply about an administration's way of redistributing a school district's professional personnel.

A Tenured Teacher:	(with fifteen years of experience) I was wondering if you could possibly reconsider your decision to furlough me?
A Superintendent of Schools:	(with five years or so of experience) You realize, of course, that there is no other viable alternative. With the tremendous drop in enrollment there is simply no need to keep you on any longer.
ATT:	I know, sir, but two years ago you told me that if I became a 3/5 teacher, my job would be secure.
ASS:	That was two years ago.
ATT:	I know, but last year you told me that if I took over the In-School Suspension Room…
ASS:	That was last year. We have to be flexible. I'm sorry you can't understand that. Now if you had dual certification, we could probably find a nice niche for you in the coming year.
ATT:	I do! I do! I'm certified in English.
ASS:	Well then—it's settled. You are an English teacher.
ATT:	You mean it's that simple?
ASS:	Of course. Now all we have to do is find a non-tenured English teacher and replace him with you. No problem.
ATT:	Wow! That certainly is a relief. My wife and kids and mortgage company are going to be very happy about this.

Several months later...

ASS: Unfortunately, there are no non-tenured English teachers. There is, however, an English teacher who has only fourteen years experience and who has tied with you in points on the new teacher evaluation form. Fortunately for all concerned, this teacher has a dual certification—in English and music. She will replace the instrumental music and band director whose triple certification and thirteen years experience qualifies him to teach Algebra I and Home Economics, two-fifths and three-fifths respectively.

                       Now the algebra teacher can be three-fifths, with the other two-fifths being physical education plus the lacrosse supplemental. The three-fifths phys. ed. teacher will take on playground supervision and p.m. bus duty. The full time paraprofessional on bus duty will be one-fifth Problems of Democracy and three-fifths Supervisor of Social Sciences.

ATT: Gee, Superintendent of Schools, you're fantastic!

"Hey, Tony! Did you finish your department budget?" That from Stosh, asked only because he had finished his.

"Yes," I lied. "I finished it last week." What I did instead was write a newsletter article that I called:

PROCEDURES: A PARABLE
"THE MOST UNKINDEST CUT OF ALL"

Once upon a time there went out a decree from Caesar Augustus that all teachers should begin ordering materials for 1973-74. Now those who had been around for a while were reluctant to do so. But those that were new and still budget-naïve began leafing through publishers' catalogs, jotting down titles and totaling up sums. Alas, they knew not what they were doing.

But the Administration would make it perfectly clear to them and to the old timers. The Administration would explain **THE PROCEDURES**...

> Principal: All right, I know you're in a hurry to get out of here so let's get started. First, all capital outlay requests are due in my office tomorrow morning.

CHRISTMAS MIRACLE

Most male married teachers with kids back in the day didn't look forward to vacations or breaks. Time off from school just meant more time at their *other* job. I was doing a little in-door house painting one particular winter break. It was in a house outside the boundaries of Facade Area School District to escape the humiliation of painting in the home of one of my students. I used the extra money to see to it my kids had a better Christmas than I ever had.

At the end of the day I rolled up my tarps, folded my ladder, cleaned my brushes, and headed home...visions of sugar plum fairies...

You could smell it all the way down the street. Turpentine. And the closer you got to Borzoni's house, the surer you were of its origin. Borzoni suffered from arthritis which lodged in his wrists. He screamed in pain and cursed his namesake St. Gennaro. He screamed in pain and cursed *MY* namesake. In fact he'd curse anyone's namesake that happened along when the pain shot through his arm and curled up his fingers. I always thought my grandfather was acting and I think he sensed my skepticism by singling out St. Anthony for an extra dose of vitriolic vituperation.

Borzoni took no stock in doctors. He took care of himself and had an asshole for a patient. What he'd do on occasion was to get a bucket and fill it a third of the way with turpentine. He'd put it on the gas stove and heat it. When it began to bubble, he'd put a *mapene*...that's what we called a dishtowel...over his head and lean over the boiling brew sucking in the toxic vapors. With every deep breath he would bleat *Madonna mia* then stand upright, the *mapene* pulled from his bald head and draped on his shoulders, and seeing me, curse up a storm. He claimed a 95% success rate and even asked me if I wanted a whiff.

That *mapene* reference reminded me of my linguistic roots. It was "gutter Italian," an expression I learned some years into my adulthood when I went off to night school to learn more about my noble Mediterranean heritage. The teacher, Mrs. Ginsburg, asked if any in the class could speak Italian. I raised my hand. She told me to say something. I did. Her response was, "Oh, you speak gutter Italian." Who knew? I thought what we heard at home was right. I never factored in that I was listening to and imitating folks who had little or no formal education. There were more mice in Borzoni's house than there were books.

Here's what I'm talking about. We had about fifty plants that lined our vegetable garden and bloomed profusely in shades of pink and white. We called them pie-knees. For years, nay forever, we called them pie-knees. My sister brought some to school once. She told Sister they were pie-knees from our yard. Sister laughed and told the entire class they were peonies. My sister cried but learned her lesson quickly. What you say at home stays at home.

It was a jolt to learn that the *scood-a-macaroon* was really a colander...that *jevella* water was really bleach...and that my grandfather was not only full of shit but also misinformation. He packed things in *cartoon* boxes. He smoked *Salaam* cigarettes. He liked his spaghetti *eye-a-oy-ya*. By God! The man was trilingual, fluent in gutter Italian, broken English, and battered Borzoni. I was being raised by a Renaissance Man.

I was always a careful observer. I could tell that all my friends down the street had more than I did. For one, they had fathers. I wanted a father desperately. I remember crying into my pillow at night asking my father why he had to die. I remember latching on to everybody else's father to take the place of mine. The men who had cars...they called them *machines*...would drive to Valley Forge to get spring water. It was free and would trickle down the side of what my young eyes saw as a mountain. I was amazed that they didn't drink from the spigot, and even more so that they would drive miles...it was less than 10 round trip...to get it.

My Uncle Joe, my father's brother, would open the trunk of his green Nash every Friday night in the summer at 7 to "go get water." His two sons tired of the trip and would always vanish when it was time to load up with empty gallon jugs. But before the trunk reached its apex, I was by his side. Uncle Joe never talked to me. He just nodded slightly. I knew that meant I could go along. Of course I had to make four or five trips to his back room to fetch the empties, but I didn't mind because I was going to ride in his car. Not just ride in it, but sit in the front seat.

Just the two of us. When we were loaded up, he'd whip out a stogie, bent from previous use, and fire up a stench that filled the machine with an aromatic cloud that still brings pleasant memories whenever I pass some ol' guys in the park playing bocce or feeding the pigeons.

Smells can do that to you…evoke memories. Where I came from it was the smell of food. You could walk up and down the street and smell what everybody was having for dinner. I always wanted what they were having in number 7 Fraley Street. That's where Uncle Joe lived with his wife and two sons and two daughters, and his mother and father-in-law. But I was never invited to dinner. I don't think anyone in the neighborhood invited anybody else to dinner. It was for family and family only. And being a nephew wasn't close enough.

I resigned myself to eating what was on my plate at home. In fact there was no choice in the matter. I find it amusing in my golden years to hear my daughter ask her kids what they'd like for dinner. And she makes them what they ask for. "*Non piace? Non mangia!*" My mother's mantra: "Don't like? Don't eat!"

We never went hungry and we never invited anybody to dinner. If I ever *was* invited, I'd probably decline because I wouldn't know how to act. There was a sameness about the menu that was more exact than the calendar. If it was *pasta e fagioli*…pasta fazool, according to Borzoni…it was Friday. Always it was Friday. Back in those days you were threatened with Hell if you ate meat on Fridays. Pasta fazool was your penance. You ate it and you offered it up. During Lent you ate it on Wednesdays too. The Sisters of the Immaculate Heart of Mary told us that knocked off days spent in Purgatory. So did scrubbing the floors in the convent.

But there were special occasions that altered the offering a tad. Christmas Eve was one. I hated Christmas Eve.

> "*Here sighs and cries and wails coiled and recoiled on the starless air, spilling my soul to tears. A confusion of tongues and monstrous accents Toiled in pain and anger. Voices hoarse and shrill And sounds of blows, all intermingled, raised tumult and pandemonium that still whirls on the air forever dirty with it as if a whirlwind sucked at the sand.*"

It wasn't just in *Dante's Inferno* that the senses were assailed. It was in Borzoni's kitchen too. I hated everything about it, especially the *smells* of Christmas Eve. Granted there were no streams of bloody gouts of pus and tears. No loathsome worms and maggots. But my young taste buds would dry into heaves come every December 24th. It was the Night of the Fishes…seven of them.

Oh please don't start gushing on about what a wonderful tradition that is until I tell you what it was like in my childhood. I blame it all on my Uncle Gus. He was from Sicily and when he came to America he brought the seven fishes with him. When he married my aunt, together they infected the rest of the family.

I always thought that one fish was bad enough, but seven was throwing salt on the gustatory wound. On Christmas Eve morning my grandfather would travel all the way to South Philadelphia's Italian Market…by bus…to buy the freshest and cheapest fish he could. It was evident that one didn't necessarily imply the other. And because there'd be packages to be carried, he'd bring me along. Passing from one town to another inching closer to the city was for me a reenactment of the Stations of the Cross. There was ignominy involved, shame of the rankest sort. I was the bearer of raw squid, smelts, and baccala. Borzoni would also get a good deal on cheese that smelled like moldy feet. That and the fish would always guarantee us a seat on the bus ride home.

What would make this night different from all other nights? Borzoni would do all the cooking. This was to honor his mother, even after she died. His holiday routine was long ago established. While my mother and aunt cleaned the fish, Borzoni would walk the three blocks up the hill to the Italian Social Club. There he would try to drink himself into the Christmas spirit. But there wasn't enough alcohol in that little town to warm the Old Man's heart. He went in a sober rat bastard. He merely came out a drunken one.

He'd stumble home, throw open the front door, and start barking out orders to all of us in the kitchen. My mother would raise her index finger to her pursed lips as a sign that we should say nothing. That was easy. I rarely said anything in Grandpop's presence. That's how scared of him I was.

He was pissed off because he only had three kinds of fish. He ranted about the significance of seven one time when my mother had the audacity to ask…for me…why there had to be seven. He grilled her in response.

"How many days in a week?"

"Seven."

"How many pilgrim church inna Roma?"

"Seven?" My mother was guessing.

"How many sacraments?"

"Okay, Pop." But there was no stopping him. He was on a roll.

"And whena the God makea the world, how long it tooka Him? *Que numero*…what number's *perfecto*? Seven! *Tutto sette*! All seven! *Capisci*?"

Borzoni had an explanation for everything. And what he didn't know, he'd make up. Like the way he used geometry to predict death. An old man across the street died, then months later one down the street died. Borzoni was quick to draw a triangle in the air that linked the two and made himself the third. "See? God makea da triang. I'ma next." Of course he wasn't, so when the next old guy died, he said God was making a square. Then a circle and then back to the triangle. When he finally did die, God had made a helix.

He made do with three fish prepared several different ways. He fried them, he baked them, he threw them in gravy. He splashed scalding olive oil all over the place. And flour and breadcrumbs. All the while cursing up a storm to welcome the Christ child into the world.

"Gosh-dons! Nun jew forgeta gosh-dons!" That's what he called chestnuts. And in true gutter fashion, that's what I called them. My sister was in charge of gosh-dons, a job she loathed the older she got. It involved partially splitting the nut with a very sharp knife. Borzoni bought a shopping bag full…because they were cheap…and insisted they be roasted as part of the feast. My sister filled three cookie trays with split gosh-dons and placed them in the oven that was set for 385 degrees. When she checked ten minutes later the chestnuts were still *raw*. The pilot light had gone out. "*Qua*," said the Old man, handing my sister a wooden match. That's when things got lively. She struck the match, opened the oven door, and set herself on fire.

Her hands flew to her face as she ran from the kitchen into the *palor*, my mother fast on her heels batting my sister's hair which was trailing a cloud of foul-smelling smoke. The Old Man joined in the chase crying out to Jesus. He tripped and fell. His cries turned to curses. "Summa bitch! Bastardo!" My mother ignored him, my sister claiming all her attention.

"Carmella! Stay still. Nun jew run. Let me see you face." My sister screamed as she turned toward my mother. My mother screamed when she saw my sister no longer had eyebrows. Borzoni continued to curse, making no attempt to get up from his prone position. "Here. Putta some butter on." She meant oleo. We never had butter. And we used to *make* the oleo by squeezing a plastic bag that had a yellow pellet in it. The more you squeezed, the more like butter it looked. Sometimes we would throw the bag to each other. Sometimes we would see how high we could throw it. And sometimes we would hit the ceiling, splatter the contents, and run and hide.

"Ma! Paul's coming tonight! Look at me! Ma-a-a-a-a!" Paul was my sister's boyfriend and he was coming for dinner for the first time.

"You looka nice. Nun jew worry." My sister turned toward me, her face glistening with oleo.

"You looka bald," said I and ran back into the kitchen tripping over the Old Man who had fallen asleep on the floor.

"Ma-a-a-a!" bleated my sister as she ran upstairs to see for herself in the bathroom mirror.

"En-doe-knee, helpa you granfath."

"He's sleeping."

"Mah, wake 'im up! We gotta clean uppa da place."

I kicked the Old Man in the leg. No response. I kicked harder. Emboldened, I kicker higher. He lifted his head and looked at me with blood-shot eyes. *"Mi piace il vino."*

"No more wine for you, Pop. It's time for dinner." My mother grabbed one arm and I the other as we tried to lift the Old Man. From upstairs my sister's spine-tingling screams could be heard.

"Ma-a-a-a-a-a-a! I'm bald!"

My mother smacked the back of my head. "See? See what you did? Bigga mouth!"

Darkness fell. The stars came out. And my sister's boyfriend showed up early enough to see for himself what life was like on the other side of the tracks. Paul was like that guy Jim in *The Glass Menagerie*, an emissary from the *REAL* world. I worried that this might be his Last Supper.

My mother foresaw that the suitor might not be too crazy about the fare so she threw some Mrs. Paul's fish sticks into the oven. She giggled at the irony. "En-doe-knee, Paul....*Mrs*. Paul."

"Yeah. very funny, Ma. You should go on Ed Sullivan." Another shot to the back of the head.

We ate in the kitchen. Borzoni, semi-sober, sat at the head of the table. To his right sat Paul, then my sister. My mother and I sat on the other side. "Can we wipe on these?" I asked holding up cloth napkins I had never seen before. My mother gave me a look and a pinch.

Paul was quite the gentleman. He never screwed up his face at the smelts which stared up at him from his plate. He never gagged on the calamari, never choked on the baccala. He even tried to engage the Old Man in conversation. He told him where he worked, what he did, what he liked. That kind of stuff. Borzoni looked him in the eye, confounded by the guy's cordiality.

cringed at all the noise but had no clue what was really going on there. But it was different. That was the important thing. It was **different**.

Day after weary day school is the same. It is deadly in its sameness. From the opening pledge of allegiance to the innocuous end-of-the-day announcements, routine is the byword. Kids are hungry for diversion. So are some teachers. That's why they came up with field trips.

I only planned one in my long tenure but it was so disastrous that I washed my hands of them for years after, only going along as reluctant chaperon when no one else could be found. Here's the story…

Dame Judith Anderson wanted to fulfill an acting dream of her lifetime. She wanted to play Hamlet. Coincidentally we were studying *Hamlet*. All right, we were reading it. Okay, okay, we were *listening* to it on records. But I was really getting into it. I enthralled my students with my own rendition, complete with swashbuckling sword play with my yardstick. We even hurled Shakespearean insults at one another.

"You wayward toad-spotted varlot!"
"Oh yeah? Well you're a mewling fen-sucked harpy!"
"Your mom's a pox-marked maggot-pie!"

When epithets turned maternal, I always called a truce.

"We need to *SEE* this play, kids. It's going to be in Philadelphia. Who'd like to go? It's a day off from school." Yes, it was unabashed pandering. All hands shot up. I was psyched. During my free period…make that planning period, teachers have never been *free* of anything…I made contact with the theatre's box office. Other teachers in my department wanted in on it so I asked about a special rate for 180 surly adolescents. The price I was quoted was $5.00…for orchestra seats. I asked for that to be repeated. "Yes," the lady said, "$5.00." What a deal! I put a hold on a block of tickets and promised to send a check by the next week. I printed up permission slips, got four other teachers to go along, and told the kids this would be an unforgettable theatre experience they'd tell their own kids about.

The kids must have been desperate for time off because most brought in the slips and the money the very next day. When I had it all, I sent off a check. Several days later a guy named Moe called from the theatre box office saying that a mistake had been made. In fact, I was quoted the balcony rate, not the orchestra rate. Those seats were going for $25 a pop. And when would he be expecting a check for the difference…GULP! $3,500! I told him he'd be expecting it when hell freezes over. I went off on a righteously indignant tirade that included suffering children and the need to keep the performing arts alive in the next generation.

I was in the main office…teachers don't have their own phones; in fact, only a privileged few have their own rooms…and I was lathered up. Gathering support from the secretaries and school visitors just passing through, I made it clear that if we did not get the seats promised and paid for, I would take this to the Better Business Bureau and the local newspaper. I basked in nods of approval and approbation although I had no clue what the Better Business Bureau had to do with anything. The guy named Moe reluctantly acquiesced. My kids were going to the theatre, and they were going to sit in the orchestra. God was in His Heaven and all was right with the world. Not quite. Read on.

We would leave after homeroom and return in time for the kids to take the bus home. There would be no time to stop for lunch so we told the kids to brown bag it. They could eat on their way back to school. In the meantime I whipped the kids into a Shakespearean frenzy. I built up Hamlet the man to dazzling heights. "Wait till you see," I said over and over.

We arrived in the City of Brotherly Love without incident. The kids entered the theatre without incident. However, it became clear before the opening lines were delivered that some miscreants had smuggled in their lunches and were already eating their odoriferous hoagies. Several rows of blue and purple-haired matrons who sat in the very front turned in the direction of the emanating onions. Their eyes heaped scorn on me and my colleagues. My own stayed riveted to the playbill.

The Ghost did a good job of spooking the kids. It was time…Scene II, enter the King, Queen, Polonius, Laertes, Voltimand, Cornelius, Lords, Attendants and…drum roll here…Hamlet. A Hamlet I had never seen the likes of. She was short and she was skinny. Her knobby knees poked through her baby blue leotards. I had never seen the Dame in anything but a dress but here she was in all her glory packing a sword that had her tilting to the starboard. There was some quiet laughter behind me but it dissipated when I turned and gave them THE LOOK…Every seasoned teacher has one. And sometimes it actually works.

The Dame went on about her princely business but she was not measuring up to the picture I had painted of her. The students were growing restless. So were the blue-haired old ladies. The noise was growing. Some of it was paper bags, some of it cellophane wrappers, some of it giggling. It reached the stage. And that's when something rotten hit the set of Denmark. The Dame stepped out of her character and strode to the edge of the stage. She raised a mailed arm as in salute and shouted, "Children! Be quiet!" Then she slowly turned and was the Prince once more. I was beyond mortification. When the old ladies turned to shake their heads at me, I turned as well and told them I was glad those kids weren't from *MY* school. I vowed never again.

Years later when I was transferred to the newly created middle school, I was talked into being a chaperon for the 8th grade trip to New York. The teacher in charge had planned everything to a T, even rest stops. We encouraged the kids to at least try. The stop was the last on the New Jersey turnpike before the New York tunnels. After each stop, no matter how brief, the conscientious chaperon takes roll to make sure we're still traveling with the same batch. Because I had the *problem* bus, I was missing one. I went back into Howard Johnson's, first looking in the gift shop and then the men's room. I looked under the stalls but saw no feet. I turned to leave when I heard sobbing. I peeped into one of the stalls. And there was my missing kid with his feet up so no one would know he was in there.

"What's the matter? Are you sick?" It was obvious that he was and that he had not gotten to the stall fast enough. He had messed his underpants. What was I to do? One hundred and fifty kids were waiting in a caravan of buses. I gave him wet paper towels and instructed him to clean himself up. I threw away his shorts. Together we made our way back to the bus.

We took off and reached the tunnels. That's when some kid in the back yelled out: "What's that smell?" His question was quickly picked up by the others who yelled,"Whew! Gross! Ugh!"

I had to do something. "All right everybody. Check your shoes! Somebody walked in something back there." I rubbed my shoes back and forth in the aisle and 48 middle school kids did the same.

We got to the city. Our first stop was at a book publisher's. God knows why we were taking middle school kids to a book publisher's but we did. My shortless friend needed to visit the men's room…in a hurry. While the tour continued, I took this kid downstairs to a dingy looking lavatory. We needed a key to get in. He ran into one of the stalls and cried even harder than the first time. He had soiled his jeans…big time. What the heck was I supposed to do now?!

I told him to give me his pants, which he did. I took them gingerly over to one of the sinks. I hit the soap dispenser and went to work on those jeans, rubbing and rinsing, rinsing and rubbing. I was in shit up to my elbows.

They still smelled rank but they were wearable…except of course that they were soaking wet. I looked over to my left. There was a blower on the wall. I walked over with the dripping jeans, unfurled them, and hit the blower with the palm of my hand. Hot air. But it only lasted a few seconds. I hit it again and again and again. The kid was sobbing in the stall. That's when I heard a key turn in the door and some old guy walked into the men's room. He looked at me...long and hard. He turned toward the sobbing stall and the half naked kid and then back to me.

"You're disgusting!"

He left before I could explain. The jeans could not be dried and they could not be worn, at least not in polite society. The kid needed new jeans. Now this was back in the 70's and teachers didn't have the proverbial two cents to rub together. I went out into the hall...keeping my foot in the door lest I got locked out...and told another teacher that someone had to go buy this kid some jeans. Well, we could find no clothing stores in this part of the city, just book publishers. Somebody remembered seeing a thrift shop around the corner so we gave him twenty dollars to bring back some pants as fast as he could. Note that it took four of us to come up with the cash. One teacher had a roll of dimes. I'm telling you, times were tough.

I got the kid cleaned up and nobody else came in. I'm sure the word was out that some pervert was down there molesting a minor. A fellow teacher knocked on the door and passed me the jeans. Even by 70's standards these were so uncool and so stiff they could stand on their own. The kid put them on. I gave him a little pep talk. "Nobody'll know...this is our secret. Okay? Now let's go to the Statue of Liberty." The ship was full, the sun was beating down on us, the wind was whipping through our hair like Peppermint Patty. That's when that same damn kid said: "What's that smell?" And that's when I vowed that this trip would be my last. This time for sure.

The next morning, a very early Friday morning before school had even started, this lady showed up at my classroom door with a homemade apple pie. She was the kid's mother. "Here," she said. "Not even my husband would have done what you did yesterday."

Most teachers would have done the same. That's just the kind of people that we are. But diarrhea is one thing; teenage bed hopping is quite another. There was no way I was going to be responsible for 150 raging adolescent hormones. I'd rather teach *The Scarlet Letter*...or be run over by a truck. There's not much difference.

It's Good for Your
Bowels

Spring was just another season I didn't look forward to when I was a kid. When other young men's fancies turned to baseball and girls, mine turned to "chi gaud eees." It was gutter Italian for dandelions. We ate them in soups and salads. And we never ever bought one in a store. We'd go out and pick them. Any field anywhere. We ignored Posted and No Trespassing signs. My grandfather, the Chi Gaud Eee King of the neighborhood, grabbed me and some *Acame* shopping bags and announced that it was time to harvest the universal weed.

"En-doe-knee, andiamo. Hurry uppa. Nun jew be da last to picka chigaudees."

"I don't like chigaudees." I might as well have said I didn't like the Holy Virgin Mary.

"Whatta you mean? You doan like-ah? Mah sure you like-ah. Everybody like-ah. Chigaudees good for your bowels." When I was a kid I didn't know what 'bowels' were. But Borzoni and his kids, in fact all the adults in my family and in my part of the world, knew of the medicinal effect dandelions had on the bowels. So did spinach and endive and anything else green and bitter. I hated the taste but more I hated being seen bent over in somebody else's yard picking dandelions and tossing them into the *Acame* bags. The other kids in the neighborhood, though, were always sympathetic.

"Hey Ant! You lose somethin'?" In fact yes—my dignity, but I didn't know what that was either. "Get your fat ass out of my yard. You're makin' shade on our tomatoes."

Usually I'd stay bent over and give them the finger between my legs.

Borzoni was ahead of his time. He would smile knowingly today if he saw the full-page ads proclaiming:

Amazing new herbal cleansing formula flushes out the harmful, energy-draining fecal matter decaying inside your body.

"See? What I toll you? Chigaudees! Now shut uppa and pick. *Andiamo!*"

If my grandfather didn't take a good healthy shit every day, he knew he was going to die. In the chigaudee-less days of winter you could hear him grunting and groaning as he strained at stool. "Summa bitch! Ah'm gonna die! *Jesu cristo mio!*" He had the common decency to do all his grunting behind closed doors, but he was loud enough to be heard all over the house. "Carmel! *Fa molto male!* Carmel!" After his blind mother died at the age of ninety, he called for my mother in times of gastric distress. "En-doe-knee! Get you mud! Ah'm gonna die! *Andiamo!*"

"Tell you granfath I no can find his enema bag," said my mother frantically searching under the kitchen sink cabinet. That was bad news and I didn't want to bear it. "*Andiamo!*" For the longest time I thought *Andiamo* was my name. That and *cuolo cavallo*, horse's ass.

"She can't find the bag," I said to the closed bathroom door.

"*Che* 'can't find'?!" Borzoni sensed a conspiracy. "*Qualcuno mi ha rubato I bagagli!* Summa bitch!"

"What's he sayin' Ma?"

"He say somebody stole his bag. Summa bitch."

There was a knock at the door. It was the Corset Man. My mother was torn between the front door and the bathroom door. "Tell you granfath to wait! Summa bitch."

"Ma said to wait, summa bitch." I enjoyed being maliciously obedient.

The Corset Man went door to door selling corsets…they never called them girdles in those days…and this was his semi-annual visit to the Borzoni residence to see if any of the ladies of the house needed to get trussed up.

The Corset Man was just one in a parade of panderers that plied their products to a captive populace. There was an Egg Man, a Bread Man, a Milk Man, and an Insurance Man. There also was a Vegetable Man but he was called the

Huckster. He had an open flat bed produce truck…fresh stuff on top, rotten on the bottom. His hand was always quicker than your mother's eye.

Oh and there was Gypper, the old guy in a horse drawn wagon that bought rags. My mother made rags. In fact, everyone in the family who could walk made rags. Rip them into strips, wind them into balls, and sell them by the pound to the Gypper who was known for keeping his thumb on the *official* scale. The buyer's only consolation was throwing rocks at his poor maligned horse. It is safe to say that you could stay in your house your whole life and just buy stuff from guys who came to your door.

Sometimes you were caught short between door-to-door guys. That's when you had to go to DeFalco's. DeFalco owned and operated the corner store and everybody went there because he accepted The Book. Every family had one. Ours was a little black one that fit easily into pocket or purse. When you bought something, old man DeFalco wrote it in his book, one of those black and white ones used in Catholic schools from time in memorial. And you wrote it in your book too. Nobody trusted DeFalco. His wife was Irish.

Money never changed hands till the end of the month. That was usually when I was sent to the store. I was the youngest and looked the most pathetic to old man DeFalco who often extended credit beyond the monthly deadline. Mrs. DeFalco, on the other hand, would peer down at me, her eyes burning into mine, and say, "You tell your grandfather to pay his bill." She'd look at the other customers and shake her thumb towards me. "He still owes from last month. And now he wants to buy an enema bag! Your grandfather's gotta lotta nerve." She majored in public humiliation.

"Ma, she wouldn't sell me one. She says he didn't pay last time. She says he gotta lotta nerve."

"*Carogna*! Nun jew marry no Irish, you hear?" She set some prunes to boiling and turned her attention and her bosom to the Corset Man. He squeezed in her gut and pushed up her bazooms, creating a shelf for her folded arms. What he did to my mother could not have been good for her spine…or her wind pipe…or her bowels.

The only good thing about Corset Day was that she couldn't bend over to pick chigaudees.

Now I have a wife who tends to my dietary needs…and my blood pressure and my cholesterol and my weight by feeding me a steady diet of zucchini and herbal supplements. Every morning I look at the pile of pills and capsules she sets on the counter next to my bowl of cereal which my grandson calls turtle food. "What's this?" I ask not recognizing a new transparent one.

"Milk thistle. It's good for your bowels."

It's Hard Being a Diplomat When Your Fly's Open

My first public school friend was Cooky Zimmerman. He had a hook nose and stick out ears. He knew lots of bad words and what he didn't know about sex he made up. He was funny, he was spontaneous, and he was crazy. He had no father, at least he never mentioned one and I never asked. Having none myself, I thought nothing unusual about his family. Except for his mother. She was a compulsive saver. She saved everything. She had newspapers and magazines piled floor to ceiling in the living room. That was the only room Cooky ever showed me. There was a path from the front door to God knows where. I never asked because I never invited Cooky inside my house. I think I was ashamed of it.

Cooky lived on the other side of town and I would always walk the 1.5 miles to his row house. Although his house had steps leading to a front porch, I would stand in the middle of the sidewalk and yell, "Yo, Co-o-o-o-ky!" This was done no more than three times with pauses in between and increasing volume. If no one came to the door after three yells, you went home. That's what all the kids did. All except Cooky. He would yell until he got hoarse or it got dark...whichever came first.

He loved the movies and knew everything about them. Not only stuff like the names of directors and producers, but also what grips and gaffers were. He came to the door after the second yell. "It's about time, you asshole. We're gonna miss the friggin' cartoons." He was the only kid I knew who said bad words in front of adults. I was a closet curser.

He always tossed questions at me to make me feel uncomfortable. "You comb your hair with a towel? You get them pants from Bucci's? Do they have a back?" Bucci was the only Italian undertaker in town. Clothes that lacked style but had lots of room for growth were said to come from Bucci's line of Final Wear.

Our little town had one movie theater with one screen. The marquee glorified it as The Broadway. But all the kids called it The Rat House. It was old and dirty and smelled musty, probably because it was right next to the river. Nobody I knew ever saw a rodent in there, but at least once a night some guy would yell "Rat!" and we'd all pick up our feet while all the girls would screech and squeal.

"What's that hanging out of your nose, asshole? Christ, did you wet yourself? Spill gravy on your shirt again? Zipper's down." Cooky was relentless. To survive time spent with him you had two choices: check everything he called attention to or ignore everything he said. I opted for the latter.

We got there before the feature started so we could find good-looking girls and sit behind them. I liked the ones with long blond hair. Cooky liked the ones that were breathing. This was our lucky night. Two beauties and two seats behind them. We slid into place, me on the aisle. Mine...I thought of her as *mine* already...was scrunched down with her long blonde hair flowing over the back of her seat. I leaned back in my seat as well...even though there were always warnings of catching ringworm if you put your neck on the headrest. As I remember there were also warnings that swimming before Memorial Day would cause polio and sitting on cold concrete would cause hemorrhoids. We called them 'piles.'

I looked cool. I also looked down. That's when I discovered that Cooky wasn't yanking my chain. My zipper *was* down. But it was dark in there. No embarrassment. Just a quick zip up and everything would be all right. All right until my beauty tried to sit up and realized she couldn't because I had cleverly zipped her hair in my fly.

"Shit!" We said together.

"Ouch!" she said alone.

"Wait," I whispered. "Don't pull; we'll work it out slowly." Cooky thought I was getting lucky and started making some animal noises. I shushed him and asked my beauty to step out into the aisle. The theater was pitch black...the scene on the big screen was a moonless night. The timing was perfect. What I did was I stood up bent forward and she stood up bent backward as we inched our way into the darkened aisle, slowly working her hair out of my fly. Then the Director said 'Let there be light' and there was...

"Asshole! Didn't I tell ya?"

Years later a similar day of infamy would befall me. It was a Thursday, my Interview Day. My Three Thousand Dollar Day. I had applied for the position of Supervisor of Language Arts, a job that would add three big ones to my shrinking salary and my growing family. I don't remember too much about my classes that day except for one unusual incident. I called a student, Paul Murdoch, up to my desk to return his composition. He took it from me and put a corner of it into his mouth. And then, without benefit of hands, he began to work the entire paper into his mouth. He chewed and swallowed it before my unbelieving eyes, turned to the class, and burped. I picked up a sheet of newsprint and wrote Dessert on it and passed it to Paul who said thanks and quickly devoured it. And then everybody wanted to get into the act.

"Make him eat this," said a classmate offering an aluminum foil snowball.

"Nah, it hurts my teeth," belched Paul.

"How about this?"

"That's a math book, Joseph."

And then it was 2:30, and my pits started to get damp. I went into the men's room to tap a kidney and comb my hair. I checked my evil eyes, pushed some stray nasal hairs up into my nostrils, and washed my hands. I looked pretty good, Millicent Snard not withstanding.

I arrived at the Administration building at 2:50 and was greeted by the Personnel Director, Mr. Dowager. I was uneasy about meeting him face to face because he had been the target of so many of my union newsletter barbs. He was the school district's chief negotiator against the teachers so I'd throw in filler like this:

Did you hear the one about the Personnel Director who won an Academy Award for his starring role in *Shaft*?

"Tony, right on time. Glad to see you," said Dowager pressing his wet and limp hand into mine. "Dr. Crater is waiting in my office." Crater was the Director of Secondary Education. I didn't know he was going to be there too but at least I had never attacked him in print. As a matter of fact, he defied attack. He was a thoroughly honest man. No shit. An honest man who got to be an administrator and was able to *remain* honest. I admired him; most other teachers in the district did too. But he talked too much. In fact, he talked so incessantly and so rapidly that he earned the epithet 'Bullet Bob.'

"Mr. Dowager. Dr. Crater. How are you?" I said sitting in the chair offered me.

"Tony, we'd like to go over your application with you and ask you a few questions. And you can ask us questions too. Okay?"

"Fine," I said. And it's a good thing I did too because that was the last word I uttered for the duration of *their* interview.

"Tony, suppose you tell us a little about your course work in Reading," said Dowager.

"You know, Tony, we're talking about K-12 here. Your course work will have had to run the gamut," interjected Crater.

"And really, we're not just talking Reading, we're talking Language Arts," said Dowager.

"Right, Bill. Language Arts is the new term but reading is still its biggest component," replied Crater.

"True, Doctor, and I guess what we need is a man who knows reading from the bottom up. So, Tony, do you favor one reading program over another?"

"Well now, Bill, I'm sure Tony realizes that there is no one way to teach reading. He knows that there are merits in most…as well as deficiencies. He probably favors an eclectic approach to the teaching of reading which could be quite compatible with the variety of approaches now in use throughout the district. Maybe I'm putting words into your mouth, Tony, but I'm sure you can see benefits and advantages in our Open Court program as well as our Scott-Foresman. Not to mention…"

"Is the Scott-Foresman the one where the teacher holds up a card?" asked Dowager.

"Tony, you correct me if I'm wrong, but I think you have a basic phonemic system in mind, Bill. Isn't it right, Tony, that this more or less involves rote memorization? Too bad our language isn't 100% phonemic. This would be simple then, wouldn't it? We'd just have to worry about a few remedial cases then, wouldn't we?" asked Crater who was impressing the hell out of Dowager.

I just sat there looking at my lap. That's when I noticed my zipper was down.

"But getting back to those cards, Bill. One of the first such was the Bremner-Davis Phonics. Maybe you're familiar with it under the title *Sound Way to Easy Reading*. It uses four phonograph records which provide classroom drill in what is claimed are 123 basic phonemics."

"Wow! How do you get so many phonemics out of our 26 letters?" asked Dowager.

"Well, Bill, it doesn't work quite that way. I'm sure Tony here is familiar with Robert Aukerman. Correct me if I'm wrong, Tony, but I think he was the one who said that phonemics is the broad term referring to systems of reading that pay special initial attention to presenting the sounds of language matched with the graphemes, with subsequent efforts to synthesize those sounds into whole words. Right, Tony?'

I nodded again and put my folded hands in my lap. I thought that with one hand over the other, I could surreptitiously yank up my zipper. It was stuck.

"I never thought of it quite that way, Doctor…compromise in action. I'll have to remember that."

"Well, Bill, I'm sure compromise is a great part of your day as Personnel Director."

"Yes, it is, Doctor. A great part…"

It was my tie. My tie was too damn long and the tip of it was caught in the zipper teeth. And my tie was yellow. Bright yellow. I showed up for a three thousand dollar interview with a bright yellow tie sticking out of my fly. I crossed my legs—faggot style—(like I said, political correctness had yet to be invented) and listened to the two *diplomats* interview each other.

"How do you think you'll be able to get on with the veteran teachers, Tony?" asked Dowager.

"Well, Bill, I'm sure age is no consideration here. Even though Tony is young—how old are you, Tony, 28, 29? Age is immaterial. I mean, real diplomacy transcends age."

"That's good, Doctor…transcends age. I never heard it worded that way before. So what you're saying is that Tony's ability to compromise will see him through encounters with, shall we say, older teachers."

"Exactly," smiled Crater.

I smiled too as I casually spread my hand over my crotch.

"Do you have a supervisory certificate? There's no mention of one in your scholastic file," said Dowager who, I think, glanced at my hand. He probably thought I was playing with myself.

"You know, Bill, we're being very lenient about those certificates. As long as Tony is enrolled in a program that will eventually yield such a certificate, there's no problem."

"Then I guess that's it, Tony. Do you have any questions you'd like to ask us?" said Dowager…to my hand.

"Maybe you should tell Tony that there are eight other applicants and that three more have yet to be interviewed…"

"We have eight…"

"And the entire process is a rather long one because we want to do a thorough screening. You'll probably be hearing from us in two weeks. One way or the other, right, Bill?"

"Yes, one way or the other. You'll certainly be hearing from us, Tony."

Then both Dowager and Crater rose from their seats and extended their right hands for me to shake. I stood, legs close together, and shook one hand and then the other. My left hand buttoned my jacket and then shot into the pocket that held my car keys. I thought that would look natural. And it would have too if I had selected the right button.

"Tony, it was nice seeing you again. I think we've all learned a lot from this afternoon's give and take session," said Dr. Crater.

He was right. I learned that it's hard being a diplomat when your fly's open.

On the way home I told the rearview mirror all the things I should have said. I stopped for a red light alongside a bus. I looked out my window and saw two old lady passengers looking down on my bright yellow tie sticking out of my fly.

I smiled and waved.

That's what Cooky Zimmerman would have done. What a diplomat he would have been!

WHAT'S IN A NAME?

Ask any teacher who is expecting a baby what their first and biggest quandary is. It's the baby's name. Picking a name is difficult for all parents, but for teachers it's almost impossible. I interacted with 150 kids a day, thirty at a time. I associated good and bad behavior with a name. *Fred* was bad; *John* was good. *Beth* was a whiner; *Sally* was annoying; *Lisa* was sweet.

My wife said that I could name all our sons, and she would name all our daughters. And there was no way she would name any of them Carmella. She settled on *Lori* and left it to me to explain the choice to my mother.

"Lori? What kima name is Lori? Theysa no saint name Lori.

"It's pretty, Ma. Lori, Lori, Lori. Sounds like you're singing. Try it."

"*Che* sing it! *Assunta!*" she said. "Singa that! Philomena, Maria, Josephine, Carmella." She raised her eyebrows as well as her voice. "Carmella, Carmella, Carmella. Atsa nice song, no?"

"No, it's going to be Lori."

"Atsa your idea or your wife's?"

"Mine. All mine."

"And what's the *priest* gonna say?"

She had me there. Those were the days when the Church was still able to get into all your business from the bedroom to the bassinet. You had to get married in the church. If you were both Catholics, it had to be with a Mass. If one was not a Catholic, no mass for you. Just a quickie recitation of vows then off to the reception. But right before that the heretic half had to promise…in writing…that all children would be raised Catholic. Oh, and the babies had to have *Christian* names.

"Her middle name is going to be Ann."
"Anna?"
"No, Ma. Just Ann."
"With a *e*?"
"Lori Ann. Two words. No *e*."
"You sist' do the sama thing. *Bren*. What kima name is Bren?"
"BrenDA, Ma. Bren***DA***."
"Yeah, I know. I gotta sing, right? Mah, go head. Name your baby Lori." On the surface she seemed to resign herself to it. But I knew she'd call her Carmel when she thought no one was listening.

When my wife announced that she was pregnant for the second time, she reminded me that the same deal was still in effect.
"What'sa name gone be? Zelda? Zelda ***ANN***?"
"Very funny, Ma. I always said you should be on TV. It's going to be Diane. It's Greek. A Greek goddess."
"Greek? *Madonna mia*! ***Greek***?"
"Yeah, and her middle name is going to be Marie."
"Maria?"
"Don't even start."

After five unfertile years went by, my wife made the surprise announcement. "We're having another baby."

Same deal with the names. I had selected Daniel and never got a chance to use it till now. "Ma, it's a boy. Daniel."
"Atsa saint?"
"Daniel. You know. In the lion's den? It's Jewish."
"Jewish?! Are you craze?"
"Ma, Jesus was Jewish."
"Sure, and look whata happen him!"

You had to keep a close eye on my mother. Not just with names but with ears. Like I told you, she was *hard of hearing* and because so many others in her family were too, she was always afraid that her kids' kids would be *hard of hearing* as well. So it was not surprising to see her quietly creeping up to the crib armed with two pot lids which she slammed together like a concert cymbalist. The baby would jerk, jump, twitch, and scream in panic. My mother would smile broadly, bless herself, and thank God.

"Atsa good, Carmel," she'd coo to Lori. "*Grazie dio*! You can hear."

"...And You Get the Summers Off

Fifteen million dollars for a five-year contract. A four million dollar bonus just to sign to play football...yup! That's America, all right. That heart stopping news was in the same edition of my daily paper that carried The Schools' Report Card. THAT story had THIS as a lead in:

Teachers hold the key to a lifetime of learning. Urban or suburban, elementary or high school, they inspire, guide and challenge their students. The rewards, they say, are rich.

Bullshit! The only thing the teachers are left holding is the proverbial bag. Now it's called *accountability*. Everything's our fault. Makes no difference that we work ten to twelve hours a day. All taxpayers see are the six and one half hours we spend with kids in the classroom. They tell each other at their country clubs that the teachers have a *cake* job. On their yachts they pine about the long hours it takes for them to make their ends meet. Oh, yeah and we get the summers off. That's what sticks in their craw more than anything.

Why don't we have the ***Dentists'*** Report Card? Why shouldn't *they* be held accountable whenever I get a cavity? If I get more than two a year, shouldn't they be put on a list warning them that if they don't make adequate yearly progress, the state will take over their practice? Same thing for proctologists. If my polyps grow back, isn't it their fault?

Back to the money thing. I spent 40 years listening to that old song: Tony, you knew that when you went into teaching you wouldn't make a fortune. And for forty years I've been singing, why the hell not? Some kid I taught tried to explain it to me.

"Mr. Angelo, who would pay 50 bucks to watch you grade papers?"

"Pardon me, young man?" That's what I always said when I couldn't come up with a fast and clever repartee.

"Imagine this," said the smart ass kid. "You're up on stage seated behind your coffee-stained desk with the broken middle drawer. You can barely be seen over the mountain of essays and term papers. A coin cup from Harrah's Casino in Atlantic City is bursting with Uniball red pens, micro point. A hush falls over the crowd as the grading begins.

"The announcer speaks from off-stage—

'Ladies and gentlemen, the close reading has begun. Angelo is moving in for the first mark of the day...*their* is misspelled. No comma after the noun in direct address. (A pattering of applause) Now a comma splice, now a missing comma, now too many commas. Oh this kid's paper is starting to suck! Wait! What's this? No genitive modifying the gerund? (*Ole!* From a kid in the bilingual class)

'Angelo is moving on to page two writing blood-red notes in the margin. Our overhead camera is able to pick up some of them. This one says...It's not nice to punctuate for the hell of it. Here's another...Don't look now but I think you turned in your rough draft. On the bottom of the page it looks like Angelo has simply written HUH? (The applause grows. The audience is getting into it.) Librarians dressed in caps and gowns with **Grade This** emblazoned on their chests lead the crowd in cheers.

Two bits
Four bits
Six bits
A dollar
All for failing this kid,
Stand up and holler!

"The Announcer joins in." The smart ass continues.

'Ladies and gentlemen, I've never seen anything like it before. Angelo doesn't miss a trick. Ouch! He's circled a dangling modifier. Now a run-on, more misspellings, tense shifts. He's drawing arrows for pronoun/antecedent agreement. His red pen is quicker than the eye.' (That's when they'd do instant replay in slow motion.)

"The *cheerleaders* chant, "Give me an A.""
The smart ass is really enjoying himself. "The audience responds at the top of their lungs *no way* as Angelo holds up a completed paper with a big fat red F scrawled across its front. The crowd goes wild coming to its feet as it screams 'To...ny! To...ny! To...ny!' That's when he comes around to the front of his desk and does this little victory dance as he twirls his Uniball between his ink-stained fingers...you get it, Mr. Angelo?"
I smiled with closed mouth and slitted eyes as my class took up the chant: "To...ny! To...ny! To...ny!"

And so to make more money, we took on more jobs. Lots of teachers sold stuff. The wealthy ones sold real estate. The annoying ones sold Amway and Mary Kay. One bleary-eyed guy was night desk clerk at a local motel. Another made stone jewelry. Several of the guys were weekend and summer house painters. I was a baker.
Come June I chalked up another successful school year. My union newsletter articles continued to have great impact on my colleagues.

"Know that one about being negative?"
"Yeah."
"Well, shove it up your ass!"

There was no new contract in the offing for September. In fact, a strike was certain. It was summer and I had to teach summer school in the morning and work at Dorkmann's Bakery at night.
Talk about the sweet smell of success.
Summer school was all right. My colleague Polly Purim always managed to fail enough kids during the year to ensure me summer sustenance. And, for a change, most of my students were black and farted at the drop of a pencil.
Dorkmann's Bakery was hell. But the money was good and if we were ever going to get my wife's dream house, I'd almost grin and bear it.
I had worked at Dorkmann's every summer and Christmas and Easter vacation since graduation from high school. I was an irregular, card-carrying member of the American Bakers and Confectioners Union. My official title was Vacation

Relief. That meant that I filled in for various departments when the regulars went on vacation.

Well, they weren't regulars, really. They were zombies. O.T. Grubber, for example. Everybody called him O.T. because he was always so hungry for overtime, some nights working as many as sixteen hours. O.T. and I worked in front of the roll oven, a mammoth contraption that never...*but never*...stopped rotating. It was a leavened Charybdis sucking in raw rolls and spewing out cooked or—in my case—burnt and/or flat ones. O.T. taught me all the tricks necessary for success on the job from the very beginning.

"Hi. My name's Tony."

"Fuckin' college kid?"

"Yeah. I'm gonna take your place."

"The fuck you are."

"For your vacation."

"Sheeeit!"

"What do I do?"

"Lift four of these mothers (pans holding 16 rolls) and throw 'em in the oven. Reach in and pull four of the fuckers out."

"They're heavy."

"Fuckin' college kid."

"Just throw 'em in?"

"Yeah."

Yeah my ass! I threw them in and they all collapsed as flat as a sixth grader's chest. But O.T. covered for me with the foreman.

"Christ sakes! What the hell kind of help is this? He's throwing the bastards in, for Christ's sake. Look at these flat mothers! Fuckin' college kids."

"Thanks a lot, pal."

"Sheeeit," said O.T. smiling like a son of a bitch.

Two weeks later I spelled a roll bagger, another job that tantalized the creative bents of mankind. It was assembly line work and the zombie at the head of the line was a sadist. His job was to dump trays of rolls onto a conveyor belt that went through a slicing machine and came out on a table in front of two stacks of plastic Dorkmann bags. The bags were hooked up to a contraption that blew air into them so I and the zombie across from me could easily and quickly slide eight rolls into each bag.

"Why eight," I asked my first night.

"Mind your own fuckin' business." The Sadist Zombie was a real sweetheart. He dumped so many rolls so fast that he defied belief. I'd look at the belt and see all those rolls come marching out at me and panic. There was no way I could fold four on top of each other and slide them into the bag, especially since my contraption seemed to be broken.

But the zombie across the way smiled serenely and bagged the hell out of his side.

"I don't have any air."

"Tough shit."

Some weeks nobody was on vacation. That's when Dorkmann's pulled a variation of seatwork on me.

"Dust the flour off the rafters."

I smiled. I thought the foreman said to dust flour off the rafters.

"What the hell you laughin' about? Get up there and dust." No shit. He gave me a dustpan and brush and pointed to a ladder on wheels. "Start here and work your way around to there."

"There" was way the hell over at the other end of the building.

I climbed up, straddled a beam, and started to dust. Hot air rises, remember? It was so hot up there that there was no way to control the sweat that dripped from my head. It splattered all over the flour dust, making dough balls that defied dusting. So I had to scrape first, then dust. After a while I developed a rhythm: straddle, scrape, dust, straddle, scrape, dust. I felt like something out of Sinclair's *The Jungle*.

When I got to the end of my first beam, I carefully turned around and crawled back to the ladder. Of course it wasn't there. Some fun-loving zombie had absconded with it.

"Hey pal," I yelled down at a grandfatherly baker. He turned around. "Up here." He turned around again. "Up here!" I yelled.

"Up *yours* too!" he yelled over his shoulder as he continued scraping jelly out of pans. I crawled right over him and dusted flour on his head. He looked up and yelled, "What the hell you doin' up there?"

"I can't find my *ladder*."

"Louder? What are ya, deaf?"

"*Ladder, ladder!*"

"Louder your ass. Goddamn college kids always actin' smart."

That's the day I found out Stanley was *hard of hearing*. He was also *hard of seeing*—even though he wore Coke-bottle glasses. I found that out when I watched him walk into a wall.

"Watch out for the wall," I yelled down from my perch.

"Sure you're gonna fall. You need a ladder, dumb ass," shouted Stanley as he careened into cinder blocks.

But this summer I didn't have to suffer the regulars' slings and arrows. I had arrived; I was a regular irregular—a demi-zombie. I spent a lot of time trying to cheer up the *inmates* who rarely smiled...unless they stole your ladder.

One time I tried to get a rise out of the bakers by having Fred Astaire Night. What I did was, I walked over to the roll oven and tapped O.T. on his sweaty shoulder.

"Get a load of this," I said as I sprinkled sesame seeds on the wood floor. "Tea for two, and two for tea"...tap, tap, tap..."just me for you and you for me"...tap, tap, tap..."oh how happy we will be"...tap, tap, tap.

O.T., zombie that he was, refused to look.

"Okay. How about this?" I placed the palm of my hand on the floor, slanted my body, and began going around in a Mills Brothers' circle. "Around the world I searched for you...I traveled on when hope was gone, to keep our rendez-vous..."

"Fuckin' teachers!"

Another time it was Circus Night. I'd go up in the rafters and do death-defying Charlton Heston stunts...without a net. I'd stand on a beam with one foot, hold out an arm and yell "Ta-*dah!*" For variation, I'd switch feet. "Ta-*dah!*"

But nobody much noticed. No shit. One night I slipped Dorkmann bags over each shoe and put one over my head and walked over to the foreman.

"Tony Angelo reporting for duty, sir."

"Put your hat on and go over to Cinnamon Buns."

"Oh God! Oh no! Not Cinnamon Buns! Anything but Cinnamon Buns," I whined, shuffling my Dorkmann-bagged feet over to the Devil's own conveyor belt.

This job was something out of *I Love Lucy*. All these four-inch cinnamon buns parading down this souped up belt. I stood next to three boxes, one containing glazed cherries, one, crushed peanuts, and the third, chocolate jimmies. I had to sprinkle this shit, one confection per bun, leaving the fourth bun plain, and then place all four neatly in a box before they went through the wrapping machine.

I quickly learned that once you touch a glazed cherry it becomes part of you. You can shake your hand until your ass falls off, you'll never get rid of that little red sucker. And while you're trying, the buns march on.

""Cherry, plain, peanut, jimmy. Cherry, plain, peanut, jimmy...it's a cinch," said one of Dorkmann's civil zombies.

"Hey, thanks...cherry, plain, jimmy, peanut..."

"No, dumbass; peanut, jimmy...*Peanut,* jimmy."

Needless to say, my crushed nuts got mixed in with my chocolate jimmies, and every bun was dive-bombed by at least two mashed glazed cherries. But I was oblivious to the mess—it was Wayne Newton Night.

"Well, it's cherry plain and peanut jimmy time," I crooned through my Dorkmann bag.

The next morning, after five hours sleep, I was off to summer school.

"We ain't gonna write today, are we, Mr. Rangelo?"

"We're *not* going to write today, Gomez."

"Solid on that 'cause we wrote yesterday," said Gomez.

"Today we're going to write poetry," I announced.

"You lie, Rangelo," muttered Gomez.

"To be exact, we are going to write cinquains. These are poems of five lines with special *stuff* in each line. The first line is a word for the title. The second line is *two* words to describe the title. The third line is *three* words to show action. The fourth line is *four* words to express feeling. The last line is the title again, or a word like it."

"That don't make no sense," said Gomez.

"That *doesn't* make *any* sense."

"You lyin' again?"

"Let me give you an example.

> Mr. Angelo
> Handsome, clever
> Teaching, helping, joking
> An idol to students
> Mr. Angelo."

"I seen a *dawg* handsomer than you," said an anonymous voice in the back of the room. I didn't know *he* failed the year.

"Now let's get busy and see if you can write a cinquain half as good as mine."
And they did. I offered them creative inspiration, a model worthy of emulation.
Check these out:

Mr. Angelo
Ugly Italian
Talking, walking, smelling
Always giving us zeros
Angelo

Angelo
Short and weird
Talking, walking, squawking
Dumb, stupid, smart-mouth idiot
Angelo

Gomez
Skinny jive frog nose
Thinks he's Casanova
Likes Shirl Jackson, the Black Tack
Worm.

Black
Beautiful Soulful
Hip, together, right on
Power to the people
Black.

Feet
Large, funky
Black and White
Narrow and Fat
Feet.

Anthony
Scar-Face
Jive as Sin
Feet stink like Garbage
Funky Tony

Ear
Dirty loud

Beating like Heart
Full with dirty wax
Ear

Nothing
Nothing, nothing
There is nothing
Every where I go
Nothing.

That last one was signed *Nobody* and really scared me. I had to find that kid…fast…before Dorkmann's did.

Driving home from school that day I thought there had to be more to the good ol' summertime than *this*. I mean, people were supposed to go on vacation, weren't they? And if you stretched your imagination a bit, you could say that *teachers* were people too, right? Well then, it was settled. The Angelos were going on vacation.

I always liked to go down the shore—Atlantic City. No shit. I really liked Atlantic City…my whole family did. Even my mother. She especially liked it when the gamblers took over. She and her girlfriends were monthly visitors to *Nica Ci-tee*. That's what she called it…and because she was the interpreter, so did all the other old ladies. She *made a bus;* that is, she conned 30 other retired seamstresses to shell out 12 bucks to spend 4 hours by the sea. Little Carmella called it *going to work*. Resorts would give them $7.50 for lunch and a roll of quarters for the slots. The ladies brought their own sandwiches—peppers and sausage, pocketed the quarters—the pay, and spent the afternoon on Boardwalk benches watching all the losers go by. Said my mother, "Atsa nice. *Mi piace molto*."

I loved it too. Ah! The Atlantic City waves…I liked to jump over them or have them lash at my belly while I yelled "Whooh! Whooh!" Remember, this was before New York started dumping its shit into the ocean. I liked to play in the sand too…with my kids or without them…I liked to lie in the sun, buy fudgey-wudgies, collect shells, feed gulls, walk under the Million Dollar Pier, get blisters on the Boardwalk, and listen to all those kids hawking at me to read all about Elizabeth Taylor and Jackie Kennedy. That's even where I was when Elvis died.

We always used to stay at a place on Georgia Avenue. If you've never been, that's down near Convention Hall. That's where all the Italians stayed. *Stayed* is probably the wrong word. We could never afford to really *stay* there as in *stay over* when I was a kid. All we could afford was a day room to change and kitchen privileges to make our lunch and cook our dinner. Yeah, we even brought our own food.

We usually put up at the Mafungool Guest House. It wasn't much but the owners, Stu and Lou Gotz, had clean sheets. Most of the *guests* were very old and spoke very little English. They divided their days between Guard Duty…making sure nobody ate **THEIR** stuff in the refrigerator…and sitting in front of the *hotel* watching the very young stroll by in pursuit of summer sun and fun.

"*Managio l'Ameriga!*" The old folks damned America for everything, but especially for their kids becoming Americanized. "No *scarpe!*"

"Hey, *culo cavallo*! Wheresa you shooz?"

"*Che peccato!*"

"Nun jew know you gonna hurt chouself?"

They really went to town when black people walked by. *They* weren't supposed to be there in those days. *They* were usually kept two blocks down from Georgia Avenue. Little old ladies who just came from 6:30 mass would roll down their black nylons to their ankles and roll up their black sweaters to their elbows and call the passersby ugly fatherless eggplants.

"*Managio mulignamo!*"

"*Toute brutto.*"

"*Che peccato.*"

"Hey, *culo cavallo nero!* Wheresa you fahder?"

"We're going down the shore when summer school's over," I said to my wife who was in the kitchen cataloging Betty Crocker recipe cards. She got about a million of them a month but we never had anything more exotic that chicken or hamburger.

Desserts were against her religion and a reminder of my humble beginnings.

""Your mother never made you dessert." She never made me breakfast either, another tradition my wife has upheld. As for the cards, I guess she just liked to collect them.

"Okay. We'll go to the shore. And we'll stay at that lovely guesthouse and sit out front with all the geriatrics and have a real ball. Can we pretty please have a hoagie supper at the Italian Village? Please? And can we stand for an hour and watch that skinny guy walk around the table making fudge? And then watch the diving horse? Oh, I'm so excited. I'm going to go pack right now."

That woman possessed the irony of Mark Antony. No shit.

"Okay then. Where do *you* want to go?" I asked.

"New England."
"Close enough."

And so we packed…and packed…and packed…and
"Why do we need these, Mare?" I held up a pair of boots.
"In case it rains."
"It's not going to rain."
"Tony, if you're on vacation, it's going to rain. Trust me."
"Coats?"
"New England nights are cool."
"Two pairs of shoes each?"
"You never know," she said. "Lori, bring down *all* your underwear."
"Why all of it?" I asked.
"You never know," she said.

We had just bought a new used car and this trip was going to be its maiden voyage. It was a beautiful air-conditioned turquoise Pontiac Malibu addicted to Hi-test. And it had a *very* small trunk. But all I had to squeeze into it were two large suitcases—plaid cloth—we got them with our Oh So Soft S&H green stamps (you can read about THAT fiasco in *Water, Water Everywhere*), one cooler filled with food for the day, one picnic jug of lemonade—Wylers's…2 cans for 99 cents with a coupon, one hat box suitcase, one overnight bag, two shopping bags full of shoes, four raincoats—I refused to take mine, three sand buckets and shovels, one beach blanket, five hangers full of *dress-up* clothes, and a partridge in a pear tree…You never know.

We went to bed early that night so that we could get an early start in the morning. Also, the calendar indicated this was one of our *safe times*. Catholic, remember? *Viva il Papa!*

LUP-LUP-lup-lup-lup…
My ears perked up and my eyes searched the darkness. LUP-LUP-lup-lup-lup-lup…I raised my head slowly from my pillow. LUP-LUP-LUP-lup-lup-lup-lup…
"Mare, put the light on."
"I'll shut it," she said. She was still half asleep.
"Mare, put the light on!"
"It's only raining. I'll shut the window."
"Put the light on!"

When she did, we were able to get a good look at the bat that was circling our love nest.

"Oh my God!"

I jumped out of bed exhibiting *raw* courage as I yelled, "Get out of here. Hurry up!"

"No! I'm afraid! Oh my God!" She screamed and pulled the sheet over her head.

LUP-LUP-LUP-LUP-LUP...

I ducked, my heart beating like a jackhammer as the bat swirled over my head.

"Get out of here...NOW!" My booming voice scared her more than the bat. She draped the sheet around her bare shoulders and ran out into the living room. I was close behind, slamming the bedroom door after me.

From upstairs my daughter Lori, a light sleeper to begin with, was screaming hysterically. "Daddy! Mommy! Daddy! What is it? I'm scared! Daddy! DADDY!"

"It's okay, Lori. Just stay in your room and keep the door shut," I yelled up the stairway.

"What is it? Is the house on fire? I'm scared, Daddy, I'm scared." By now she had awakened her sister Diane who was also screaming.

"Daddy! Mommy! Daddy! Mommy!"

"It's okay, girls. Just keep your door shut. There's a bat down here but Daddy'll get rid of it in a minute. There's nothing to be afraid of." I was lying my naked ass off.

"I'm scared it's going to hurt you, Daddy," screamed Lori shakily.

"Nothing can hurt Daddy," I screamed back just as shakily.

I opened the hall closet in search of something to cover my vital organs. The only things that weren't packed away were my raincoat and my boots. I put them on and ran to the kitchen to get my O-Cedar broom. My wife scooped up her sheet, now even covering her head, and ran right after me.

"Oh my God, Tony. What are we going to do?" She was now crying.

"I'm going to clobber it with the broom," I said uncertainly.

I grabbed the broom and a dishtowel. My wife grabbed an iron skillet and a frying pan. You never know.

I put my ear against our bedroom door. There was no LUPPING going on. I went into my son's room and gave it a once over. Danny was still sound asleep, oblivious to the commotion going on about him. I closed his door securely and went back to our bedroom door. Still no lupping.

"Call the fire department, Tony." (We called them one time before when our TV was struck by lightning and they smashed our front door to get in. That cost me a fortune.)

"I can take care of this myself." I was famous for words like these.

"Well, what are we going to do?"

In that instant I formulated the following daring strategy: I was going to open the front door, quietly open our bedroom door, grab my wife, and hide in the hall closet until the bat flew off into the full moonlight.

I opened our door as cautiously as the narrator in *The Tell Tale Heart*. And like him, I peeped in. There was no bat. I opened the door a bit wider...still no bat...Finally I opened the door entirely. Nothing.

"He's gone, Mare."

"Are you sure?" She was quivering.

"Of course I'm sure," I said as the bat crawled out from behind the shade and started making lupping laps around the ceiling. I ran back into the living room to find my sheet-draped wife standing in the center of the room holding her skillet aloft. She looked like a deranged Lady Liberty.

"Get into the closet," I yelled.

"Mommy! Daddy!" screamed Lori.

"Daddy! Mommy!" screamed Diane.

"Oh my God!" screamed Miss Liberty.

The bat, sensing there was a party going on, lupped into the living room.

"Duck!" I yelled as I swung my broom at the frightening creature of the night. I missed...of course...and my movement confused it. Or pissed it off. It came for me, swooped low over my head, and started its circular flight pattern again. "Fly out the door, you dumb bastard," I cried, waving my O-Cedar like a madman.

It swooped again; I swung again. Swoop. Swing. Swoop. Swing. Crash. I broke the cut-glass vase on the TV. Swoop. Swing. Crash again. A genuine Apple Tree Hummel. Swoop. Crash. A nick in the piano bench. Hell, I was going to town like a volunteer fireman!

I got a Babe Ruth grip on my broom and pointed to the door. "Okay, you mother, come at me chest high!" And it did. I connected but it was a foul bat. It bounced off the wall and landed on its back on the rug. What a tiny little thing it was. No shit. Its body wasn't much bigger than a golf ball. I felt for all the world like a mean ol' playground bully. "You can come out now, Mare. I got him."

"Are you sure?" came the voice from the closet.

"Yeah," I said as I threw my dishtowel over it.

The door opened slowly, my wife surveying the battlefield. "Is it under there?" she asked.

"Yeah."

She uplifted her skillet and swung down at the little hump. "You rotten lousy bat," she said savagely. "You rotten lousy bat!"

"Okay Mare. Calm down. It's dead."

"Daddy! Mommy!"

"Mommy! Daddy!"

"It's okay, girls. You can come down now," I said.

Holding on to each other for dear life, those poor little girls shot into the living room grabbing on to my raincoated legs. They were scared shitless. This called for Judy Garland Night!

"Ding dong the wicked bat is dead," I sang, transforming my O-Cedar into a baton and high-stepping around the dishtowel like a drum major.

Then the dawn came, rosy-fingered, and it was vacation time for the Angelos.

Next stop…Connecticut," I said as I backed out of the driveway and stalled in the street. "No problem," I said as I started up again. This time I got as far as the traffic light a block away from our house before stalling again. I was getting annoyed but my family was exhibiting their usual stoic patience.

"Didn't you get everything checked like I told you:" asked my wife.

"Is the car broke?" asked Diane.

"Put the air conditioner on," said Lori.

"When we gonna be there?" asked Danny.

"Now don't *flood* it, Tony. I read in *Good Housekeeping* that you're supposed to keep the gas pedal all the way down. You're not supposed to pump it like *you* always do."

"Thank you, Mary Ann," I said as I pumped.

"I can't breathe. Put the air conditioner on," repeated Lori.

"I think the car is broke." Ah Diane…always the optimist.

"I have to do pee pee," said Danny.

"Oh Danny! Didn't you go before we left?" asked my wife.

"I forgot," said Danny, pulling his tommy toodle.

When my wife wasn't looking, I floored the pedal…and that damn car started right up. No shit. *Good Housekeeping*.

We drove twenty air-conditioned miles without incident and then stopped at a gas station for Danny.

"This one isn't very clean," said my wife, removing a paper toilet seat cover and a can of Raid from her pocketbook. "You girls have to go?"

"I'll try," said Diane. She had a thing for tinkling in new surroundings.

And then we were on the Pennsylvania Turnpike having our premier Me First fight of the day.

"I get the ticket," announced Lori.

"Uh-huh," said Diane. "You got it *last* time. Didn't she, Mommy?"

"Just a minute. I'll check it out." She opened her pocketbook and removed a little calendar. "This is *Diane's* week, Lori."

"That's not *fair*," whined Lori. "She gets to do *everything*. I don't see why she has to get the ticket. It's on *my* side…and I'm not letting her lean over!"

"When we gonna be there?" asked Danny who had somehow managed to smuggle his sand bucket and shovel into the car.

"I'll get the ticket…and we'll be there in a few hours…and don't hit Diane over the head with that shovel!"

"Ow!"

"Danny!"

"I used the bucket." You had to be specific with Danny. "How long's an hour?"

"Sixty minutes," said my wife tossing Brach candies over her left shoulder.

"*Good Housekeeping?*" I asked.

"Erma Bombeck."

"Diane has all the vanilla." (We pronounce it *vanella* in our family.)

"Uh-huh, they're butter chews."

"I like red," said Danny. He was a great little kid. He'd eat a turd if it were red.

"Danny's throwing all the papers out the window," squealed Lori.

"Keep America Beautiful, Danny," I sloganed.

"He's gonna get arrested…You're gonna get arrested, Danny," threatened Lori.

"What's 'rested?"

"They throw you in jail."

"Is that right, Dad?" Danny was worried.

"Ask your mother."

"They do, Danny, because I saw a sign back there that said if you litter you have to pay a $300 fine and you don't have $300 so they'll throw you in jail," explained Lori.

"Is that right, Mom?"

"Why are you slowing down; this is a *turnpike*, you know," said my wife.

"I'm not slowing down, the *car* is!" I floored the gas pedal. Do you believe it? I was going a legal 55 and that damn car stalled out. On the turnpike. With cars all around us. No shit.

"Put your hazard flashers on!" shouted my wife.

"What the hell's a hazard flasher?" I asked gazing at all the knobs on the dash.

"You didn't read the manual, did you? I told you to read the manual before we left. Remember? I knew you wouldn't…that's why I read it…"

"Just tell me where it is, will ya?"

"That button on the steering column," she said as she reached over and pushed it in. "Coast over to the shoulder before we get killed."

"Why are we stopping?" asked Lori.

"Are we there? Where's the beach?" asked Danny.

"Is the car broke again?" asked Diane.

"Nothing to worry about, gang. I'll just start it right up and we'll be on our way." And, surprisingly, it *did* start right up. "Next stop…Connecticut." Well, not quite. We got as far as the Garden State Parkway in New Jersey and stalled again. "I know…I know…hazard flasher."

"Gas station, you mean," said my wife.

"Are we there *now*?" asked Danny.

"It's starting to rain," said Lori. I threw a Brach's at her.

Gas stations—like principals—are never there when you need them.

"Look under the hood," said my wife.

"What for?"

"I don't know; *you're* the man," she said. She said that a lot, especially if something distasteful had to be said or done. "What's taking you so long?"

"I can't find the catch."

"You could if you read the manual," she said cheerily.

"The hell with the manual?"

""Daddy said a bad work, Mommy," said Danny.

"Daddy didn't read the manual," said Mommy.

I got it open—finally—and looked inside. It was only the second time I had seen the motor since I bought it. It looked nice and clean.

"See anything?"

"Yeah, lots of things," I said. But I didn't know what any of them were for. "Damn schools!"

"Daddy said another bad word," said Danny who was now keeping score.

"It's raining, Daddy," said Lori.

"I know, Lori." I knew because the water was dripping off my nose.

I've been through high school, college, graduate and post-graduate school but, with the exception of reading, I've never learned anything *practical* in any of them. No shit. Would an algebraic formula help me out in a pinch like this? Or a Shakespearean sonnet? Maybe a research paper on Chandragupta?

Shouldn't the damn school have taught me what was under the hood? Not my school. And I'll bet not *yours* either. They only taught you stuff like that if you were dumb. Their definition of *dumb* was a kid who wasn't going off to college and couldn't learn to speak French. Half the world must be full of dumb kids who know what's under the hood and the other half full of smart asses like me who get soaked and wet trying to figure it out. *C'est domage!*

"Try it," I said to my wife.

"What did you do?" she asked as it started right up.

"Just a little trick I learned," I said. The *trick* was lying like a rug.

"I know," said Diane. "Next stop…Connecticut." I threw Brach's at her too.

We crossed the Tappanzee Bridge—for an outrageous buck-fifty—and were in New York. Just a few more miles and we'd be in Connecticut. Our first stop was to be the Shakespeare Theater in Stratford. My passengers weren't so crazy about the idea, but after all, I *was* an English teacher.

"I have to do pee pee," said Danny.

"You always have to do pee pee, Danny," I said.

"Yup," he said. "That's me all right." He was a cute little guy but I think he had a drop bladder.

I pulled into the first Howard Johnson's before the Connecticut Turnpike. And God sent to us a gas station and an attendant who was the nicest guy I've ever met. I explained my problem to him while my kids went off to do pee pee. Diane said she didn't really have to go, but she'd try.

"This got one of those gas filters in the tank?" he asked.

"I don't know."

"Yes, a plastic bag," said my wife fanning herself with the manual.

"Thought so. These bastards get clogged up easy."

"You said a bad word."

"Huh?"

"What's the *word*?" I said. "Can you fix it?"

"Yeah, but it'll cost you some gas." With that, he hooked up his air hose to the gas line in front, removed the gas cap in back, and blew expensive Hi-test all over the place. "That should do it," he said. "Tell you what, so's you don't take any chances, don't get on the turnpike yet, try it on that hill over there. Better yet, I'll go with you so's you don't get lost." And he did and we didn't and the car didn't stall one time.

When we returned to the station I asked the inevitable. "What do I owe you?"

"Nothing. Nothing at all. Have a good safe trip, that's all," he said as he shook my hand. No shit. No charge. What a guy. I wonder if he knew any French.

We got to the turnpike and God sent us the sun to dry up all the rain. And the inky-dinky spider went up the spout again. *That's* the kind of shit I learned in school. My wife was quick to point out that I didn't learn *that* very well either. She claimed it was itsy bitsy, not inky dinky. She took my seething silence for acquiescence.

The Connecticut Turnpike was something out of the Middle Ages but my kids thought it was great. They had these collection booths set up only several miles apart—I swore every mile but my wife said I was exaggerating—and they demanded a quarter at each one. Diane, because it *was* her week, tossed the first coin. She missed and wanted a second turn. The fair-minded Lori wouldn't hear of it.

"It's my turn."

"But I missed," whined Diane.

"Too bad," said Lori as she pinched her quarterless sister.

"Aah! Lori pinched me! Aaaah! Aaaah!"

"Aaah yourself!" I mimicked as I tossed another quarter in the pot. I missed too.

"Oh my God!" said my exasperated wife as she got out of the car, walked around, and dropped a *third* quarter right where it belonged. Let's get out of here before we get arrested for loitering."

For a minute there I thought she was going to leave the other two quarters to the great state of Connecticut. But she groveled around until she found them. "Hurry up," she said. "Can't you hear all the honking?"

We got off the turnpike and followed signs saying Visit the Stratford Theater. In twenty minutes we were there...but nobody else was. Seems they close up in August for repairs.

"Where's the beach?" asked Danny.

"Is this it?" asked Lori.

"They perform Shakespeare's plays here," I said, taking movies that only I would ever watch. A painter up on the ladder against the octagonal building turned and waved his brush at me. I zoomed in on him...he looked like one of the Henrys.

"Who's Shakespeare?" asked Diane.

"Some guy that wrote plays a long, long time ago," I said. "There's a picnic area over there. Want to eat our lunch now?"

"Might as well," said my wife.. "Didn't you read the brochure we got about this place? It probably tells you when it's opened or closed."

We ate our lunch, watched men cut grass and paint walls, walked around the grounds, took a few pictures, piled back into the car and headed for Mystic Seaport. "What'd you think?" I asked.

"Big deal," said an anonymous voice in the back.

Mystic Seaport closed at five. We got there at quarter of...in time to see most umbrella-wielding visitors leaving.

"I could have told you it would be closing. It says right here in the brochure..." I emptied the whole Brach's bag over my wife's head before she could finish.

"Well, let's just look for our motel, have supper, a good night's sleep and then go on to Plymouth. We can come back here on our way home."

"Yes, we wouldn't want to do too much in one day, would we?"

"No, *we* wouldn't, HONEY!"

"Are you going to have a fight?" asked the perceptive Lori.

"Mom and Dad don't fight; we *discuss.*" said my wife. And for the next sixty-five minutes Mary Ann and I *discussed* the route to be followed to the motel.

"Triple A is never wrong," she said.

"Bullshit," I said.

"Is bullshit a bad word?" asked Danny. He wanted to be sure before he called me on it.

Of course Triple A was right. The motel was exactly where they said it would be.

"Is this Rhode Island?" asked Lori.

"Yup," I said.

"Nope," said my wife.

"What do you mean 'nope'?"

"It's in Massachusetts."

"Daddy said it's Rhode Island."

"Well, Daddy's wrong."

"Oh sure. Daddy is *always* wrong!" I shouted.

"No you're not," she said.

"See? See what I mean?!"

"Are they *discussing* again?" Diane asked Lori.

"Bullshit," said Danny.

She got me on a technicality. It *was* Massachusetts but Rhode Island was just across the street. Our room was nice and clean—sheets *and* toilet. Mary Ann inspected the former, Danny the latter.

"Danny peed on the seat again," grumbled Diane.

"I sleep on this side," said Lori as she claimed her half of one of the two double beds.

"This is my side," reasoned Diane.

"Where's my bed," asked Danny rubbing himself.

"Leave your Tommy-toodle alone," said my wife. "And lift the seat up next time."

"Daddy said it's my peanuts," corrected Danny.

"I have breasts," bragged Diane.

Since it was raining and thundering and lightning, we decided to eat our picnic lunch on the floor.

"Is this liverwurst?" I asked.

"Shhh!"

"Liverwurst on English muffins?"

"Shhhhhhh!"

"Blah!"

"Yeech! I hate liver! I'm not eating this!"

"You had to open your big mouth, didn't you? You couldn't just sit there and eat it, could you?" scolded my wife.

"Whoever heard of liverwurst on English muffins?"

"Whoever heard of horseless carriages?"

"What does that have to do with anything?" She was reigning queen of *non-sequiturs*.

"Bless us, oh Lord, and these Thy gifts…"

"Some gifts," I whispered.

"…which we are about to receive from Thy bounty…"

"Bounty! Ha!" I snorted.

"…through Christ our Lord. Amen."

"If Daddy doesn't eat *his*, do we have to eat *ours*?" Lori was reigning queen of *quid pro quo*. Of course Daddy ate his and everybody ate theirs…with reservations and concessions. "I'll eat the English muffin but I'm not going to eat the liverwurst."

"Ooo! Sick!" said Diane after dunking hers in lemonade.

"I'll just eat the chips," said Danny from the bed…*our* bed.

"Get off that bed right now! You're going to get crumbs on those clean sheets...Don't jump off...the lemonade is...Oh Danny! Get some paper towels...Oh Danny!" shouted my wife as she crawled over to save the jug—sticking her knee in the coleslaw.

"I'm not eating the coleslaw," said Diane.

"If you don't, you won't get any dessert," said my wife automatically as she sopped up the lemonade. "These slacks are brand new...mayonnaise all over my knee...crumbs...rain..."

"There's a muffin in the toilet," said Danny who for once remembered to lift the seat.

Diane gulped down her dessert before we could torment her.

Mary Ann wasn't in a very good mood so I took the kids to the motel lobby where they emptied candy and gum machines and brochure and postcard racks. I emptied the ice machine...a deed which earned me the night manager's scorn.

"That ice is for 30 units, ya know? It won't drop another load for two hours, ya know? Everybody fillin' coolers...takin' all the brochures..."

"My daddy's a teacher," said Diane.

"It figures," said the night manager.

Back in the room we settled down to a little TV. The kids were in heaven. There was something on every channel. None of it was worth watching so they took turns spinning the dial after every commercial.

"Okay. Say your prayers and get into bed," I said clapping my hands.

"Ooo! Sick!" said Diane. "the floor's sticky on my side...Can I just stoop?"

From her dry side Lori intoned, "Jesus doesn't love stoopers." Ah! Sister Avila lives! My daughter had IHM written all over her.

"Where's *my* side?" asked Danny.

"Be near me, Lord Jesus, I ask you to stay..." I began.

"...close by me forever, and love me I pray..."

"...Bless all the dear children..."

"...In their underwear..."

"No, Danny. It's 'in your tender care,'" I corrected with a smile.

"Oops! I made a mistake," he giggled.

"And bring us to..."

"...ShopRite..."

"...Heaven..."

"Oh yeah, Heaven..."

"...to live with You there."

"Amen."

history only by accident. Mary Ann, on the other hand, was now traveling with a sedate family from Quebec, taking her good ol' time listening to the informative lecturers stationed here and there. My kids ran down the gangplank before I could take movies of them, but I got some great shots a half hour later of my wife and John and Myra and their daughters May and Ida.

After a sacrilegious romp through a nearby cemetery, we took off for Plimouth Plantation. And glory Hallelujah! My kids were impressed! There were real people doing real things—just like they used to back in the day. Men were playing ten pins, kids were rolling hoops, girls were dipping candles, ladies were churning butter. Everybody was doing something. They even invited participation.

"Want a taste?" asked a young Colonial pretty. "It's fish head soup."

"Ooh! Sick!" said Diane.

"Want to try churning?" asked another lovely.

"Ugh! It's hard. How long does it take?" asked Lori.

"A couple hours."

"We never have butter," volunteered Diane. "My mommy has coupons for margarine…"

"Want to roll in the hoop?"

"No thanks," I said.

"Go ahead, Daddy," urged Lori.

"Yeah, Tony, go roll your hoop," said my wife.

Later that afternoon we moved on to Boston. It took a while because I couldn't get off the freeway—mainly because I thought Rotary signs were club announcements.

"Tony, you're going in circles."

"Thank you, Mare."

"Daddy, you're going in circles."

"Thank you, Lori."

"Daddy, you're…"

"I know, Diane." I was now on my third revolution.

"I have to pee," said Danny.

"Of course you do."

"You must be going too fast," said my wife.

"Fast? A lousy 25. Is that fast?"

"Well, there's a police car behind us flashing its lights."

I looked in the mirror. She was wrong. There was an entire *squadron* of police cars behind me flashing their lights. "Is this a one-way Rotary?" I asked slowing down to ten.

"Oh my God! Here come motorcycles!"

"I bet they saw Danny throwing paper out the window," said Lori.

"Are they gonna 'rest me?" Danny sounded worried.

I rolled down my window and asked the officer what I had done. "Nothing, sir, but we'd appreciate it if you would quit making laps around the Rotary and get off. There's a disturbance at the beach and you're in the way."

"Thank you, officer. "I'm on my way...Put the radio on, Mare. See what the disturbance is." Turns out that this Saturday of all Saturdays for the past 200 years was the Saturday blacks were having a *wade-in* at all-white private beach clubs.

"Don't they like black people in Boston?"

"I guess not, Diane."

"Do *you* like black people?"

"Sure."

"Why didn't you marry one?"

"Cause I married Mommy."

"If you didn't marry Mommy, would you marry a black lady?"

"Maybe. Would you mind?"

"I don't know. Would *I* be black?"

"Half."

"Which half?"

"I have to pee," said Danny.

"Of course you do."

We found our motel and were surprised at the beauty of the place, especially since the rates were so low. This was the first vacation where we actually called ahead and made a reservation. It was not unusual for us to go from motel to hotel seeking the lowest rate. We were a tag team. Sometimes my wife would drive and I would run into the lobby. "How much for a room?"

"Twenty-five."

"No thanks." And on to the next one.

"Thirty."

"Whoa! That's too steep." Then it was Mary Ann's turn.

"Couldn't you make it fifteen? I've got three little kids out there sleeping in the back seat. We're neat, we're clean, and best of all we're quiet..." That's what

I told him…and he believed me. We quickly took possession before he found us out.

This place was nice. A spacious bedroom with a balcony overlooking a pool, a dressing room, a full bath with a sunlamp, and an ice machine right outside our door.

We quickly changed into our bathing suits and headed for the pool. The kids were excited but I knew what was coming—The Watch Me's!

"Watch me, Daddy," said Lori as she dived off a step.

"Watch me, Daddy," said Diane as she did a backstroke into an old woman with a beehive hairdo, who didn't want it wet.

"Watch me, Daddy," said Danny as he filled his bucket with cold pool water and poured it on the unsuspecting feet of a sleeping sunbather.

My wife already had her lounge chair pulled up to a group discussing interesting night spots. She was nodding and smiling…probably because nobody was asking her to watch anything.

"Marsha said no trip to Boston is complete without a visit to Chinatown."

"Who's Marsha?" I asked.

"Marsha Fenner. From Wilkes-Barre. She comes here every year. She said that she always goes to Chinatown for at least one supper per visit. The only time she missed was when her husband had that planter's wart on his right heel…"

"Alright…alright. I don't want to hear about their warts. Let's just go." We did but we didn't. The Chinatown we found was a porno strip. Every other building seemed to cater to a variety of Occidental and Oriental degeneracy. Sleazy-looking men walked the dirty sidewalks; women of the night loitered on the corners. Mary Ann was angry with Marsha…and no longer hungry.

"Mrs. Pearlstein goes to Anthony's Pier 7," said my wife locking the door. I didn't even ask who Mrs. Pearlstein was. I just started driving around until I found it. When I did, I realized that the Pearlsteins were far more affluent than the Angelos.

I'm not too good at vivid description when I'm awed and this place awed me. I mean I'm from humble surroundings. I'm from a family that never heard of eating your salad BEFORE your *entrée*. We ate it last…with the meatballs. And we never heard of *entrée* either. Oh and we only used one dish…for everything. We never put our napkins on our laps and we never left anything on our plates. I told you…my wife pulled me out of the gutter. I was used to McDonald's where kids and spilt milk were the rule. But this place was something else.

"Is that the parking lot?"

"No, it looks like a driveway…Yup, it's a driveway and those guys in the white suits park your car…for a small fee. I'm going to park across the street."

"We have to walk all the way up there?" asked Diane.

"It'll give you an appetite," I said.

"Can I have a milkshake and french fries?" asked Lori. See? Another generation of gourmets.

"Me too?"

"Me too?"

The dreaded answer from my wife: "We'll see."

When we finally reached the joint, we were confronted with two entrances, one seemingly to an old ship, the other with doormen letting in elegantly dressed ladies and gentlemen of obvious means. My wife was wearing a J.C. Penney pants suit with a coleslaw stain on one knee. I was wearing a safari jacket with a melted Brach's stuck to the back of it. The girls were wearing slacks and halter-tops. Danny was wearing a Winnie-the-Pooh special. But they let us in anyway.

The next part is fuzzy but to the best of my recollection the entrance was an enormous foyer leading to a magnificent mirror-lined, curving stairway. In situations like this I always get behind someone who looks like he knows what he's doing and imitate him. The gent I picked was escorting a Paris original up the stairs. Between them was a little girl with long sausage curls, ten or twenty petticoats, a pink pinafore, white anklets, and sparkling white patent leather shoes. I looked down at Diane's Buster Browns which were scuffed to the laces. It made me wonder if in fact we *were* all God's children.

"Look! That's Jerry Lewis," said Lori who could always be counted on to talk extra loud when you were trying to be extra inconspicuous.

"Sh!" said my wife.

"Here's Frank Sinatra and…"

"Not so loud, Lori. Everybody can read the pictures for themselves."

"How do you read a picture?"

"You know what I mean. Just be quiet." This was just what I needed…the eating-place of the stars.

There were several landings along the way and on each one were several tiny glass-top tables surrounded by scotch and soda swizzling swells. We just sashayed right on by them looking straight ahead. The gent I was following walked up to a microphoned lectern behind which stood a tuxedoed dandy looking over a huge book.

"Rogers," said my gent.

"Dumb job," she said, staring right into the guy's face as he filled her glass for the sixth time.

"Kid's crazy about water," I said to the smiling guy.

"Good evening. I'm Monique. I'll be taking care of you this evening. Are you ready to order?"

"Yes, we are. Two seafood combinations and three chopped sirloins...with french fries.

"You said I could have a hamburger..."

"And a milk shake."

"Me too," from under the table.

Ol' Monique smiled at me. "How did you do that?"

"I went to college."

There were a few other kids at some of the tables nearby but they were nothing like mine. I mean they were all sitting around the table, napkins on their laps, full water glasses, wearing their own clothes...the whole bit. Our food came and then the real action began.

"Where's the ketchup?" asked Diane.

"I'll get it," said Lori who leaned back and snatched it off the table behind her. My wife made her no-no faces again.

"Come on, Danny. Your hamburger's going to get cold...Danny! Danny?" I looked under the table—discreetly, of course. He wasn't there. There was some giggling from the next table, but it wasn't from the couple who were lost in each other's eyes.

"Danny, come out from under there or I'll throw you in the harbor."

"That lady has her hand in that guy's pocket," said Danny smiling and returning to his seat and cold hamburger.

"That's 'cause it's cold in here," I said returning to my combination. It was cold too.

"Lori, try to keep my sleeve out of your dish," said my wife, a note of indigestion creeping into her voice.

"Bleech! That guy poured water in my milk," said Diane. Sure enough he had. And he was smiling about it.

"Keed crazy bout wudder," the guy said, showing four rows of Assistant Paper Asshole Teeth.

"Tony, ask for the check and let's get out of here."

"Don't you want dessert?"

"I do."

"Me too."

"Me too."

"You guys didn't even finish your hamburgers."

"I don't like chopped loins," said Diane.

"Check please."

"How much, Tony?"

"Fifteen dollars," I said.

"Are you kidding?"

"Yeah, it's $53.50." Remember—this was back in the day when I was making about $6,800 a year. These restaurants aren't for teachers. Either are the designer clothes. People say that teachers are important...and vital...because they touch the future and pass the torch and all that other bullshit, but people want to keep teachers in their place. *Not* a place like Anthony's Pier. You know teachers should get more money, but then you start with the summers off crap and the six-hour day and the lousy teacher you had in the 4th grade, and before you know it, we're looking at a pay cut!

"Oh my God! Do you think they take Travelers' Checks?"

"I hope so, Mare. I only have thirty bucks in cash."

"Thirty? You said you had enough and then you take us to a place like this..."

"Monique, we're friends of the Pearlsteins...from Wilkes-Barre..."

"No," whispered my wife, "that's the Fenners."

"We're friends of the Fenners and every time they come here..."

"They don't come here," whispered my wife again. "They go to Chinatown."

"I never heard of either one," said Monique, "but Travelers' Checks are good here."

"Why did you leave money on the table, Daddy?" asked Diane.

"It's a tip," I said. "Let's go."

"What's a tip?" asked Diane.

"It's money you leave for the people who do things for you."

"Is a dollar a good tip?" asked Lori the Loud Mouth.

"Sh!"

We walked out looking like the poster family for Goodwill Industries. Diane, still wearing my jacket, descended the staircase trailing my sleeves regally behind her. Lori, having sense enough to roll Mare's sleeves up, skipped down the steps looking like a dwarf with malignant biceps. Danny had stopped under one of the glass-top tables and had his nose pressed against it to the wonder and consternation of the young martini-sipping couple seated there.

"Come on little boy," I said grabbing his hand. "I'll help you find your mommy."

All the way back to the motel my wife kept stewing about the check. "$53.50. We could have stayed here for two more days for that," she said. "I told you not to take the corn, didn't I?"

"It's all Diane's fault," I said. "If she didn't drink all the water, we could have left just like you said."

"Very funny." My wife was not amused.

"Okay, gang," I said pulling into the motel parking lot. "Straight to bed. We have to go to church tomorrow."

"We went last year," said Danny.

"Ahh. Isn't this nice?" I asked after we had prayed and tucked away the kids. "Wanna mess around?"

She snapped my Jockey shorts and said, "We have to go to church tomorrow."

"Want to at least jump up and down on the bed?" But she was already sound asleep, her mouth wide open.

"Effel?" called a voice outside our door. "Effel!...EFFEL!"

"What's that?" My wife sat up abruptly.

"Some guy yelling for Effel. He sounds drunk,"

"Well, make him go away before he wakes up the kids."

"Why? You wanna mess around?"

"Tony..."

"Okay, okay," I walked to the door and said, "There's no Effel here, pal. You got the wrong room."

"Who's in air wif ya, Effel?" Now he was pounding too.

"There's no Effel here. Now go away before I call the cops."

"Lemme in, Effel, or I'll knock the door down!"

"Oh my God!" screamed my wife.

"Aha! I heard ya, Effel. Come on, lemme in. I'm sorry...I'll never do it again...onis."

"Mommy, what's that noise?" asked Lori.

"Were you jumping on the bed again?" asked Diane.

"No, we have to go to church tomorrow," I said. And then to the door: "I'm the motel detective. Effel's in another room. I'll help you find her."

"Is she lost?" asked the door.

"Who's out there, Daddy?" said a frightened Lori.

"Nobody," said my wife. "Daddy's just practicing his ventriloquism."

"Good one, Mare."

"Know what, Effel?...You make me sick! Know that? Huh? Do ya?

"See? Daddy didn't move his lips one time."

"Aren't you supposed to use a dummy?" asked Lori.

"I thought I'd try it with a door this time."

"How do you bang on the door without using your hands?" asked Diane.

"I went to college," I said.

"Okay kids, show's over. Back to sleep," said my wife.

"I'm going out to get some ice," I winked to her. A few minutes later I came back in and said, "Effel's one floor up. I reunited them."

"You're a saint…but we're still not going to mess around."

Going to your own church with three little kids is usually not very inspiring or elevating. Going to a strange one is worse yet.

"Is that God up there?" asked Danny.

"Shh. It's a saint."

"How'd they get it up there?"

"Somebody painted it—now be quiet."

"With a ladder?"

"Yes. Shh!"

"We have a ladder."

"Yes, but you have to be quiet in church. Kneel down."

"I don't like to kneel down."

"It's good for you…and it makes God happy."

"Does God kneel?"

"Danny, if you don't shut up, you can't swim in the pool today," I said leaning over his little head.

"Don't pinch," he said, instinctively flinching. Smart kid. Mary Ann and I always pinch in church. We're *Roman* Catholics. "Here, play with Daddy's keys…and be quiet."

"Where are the guitars?" asked Lori.

"Shh! They don't have any, I guess. Kneel down," said my wife.

"Can I lean on my butt?"

"Jesus doesn't like leaners," said Diane flashing a touché grin as she kneeled ramrod straight.

"I don't like this song," said Lori.

"Shh!"

"Could I put the money in?"

"Here…here's some quarters for everybody. And don't take change," I said. I looked straight at Lori mainly because she came out ahead every Sunday.

"Where's the man with the basket?" asked Diane.

"Shh! They don't have a man here. They just pass it along." I said.

"They had a man last year," said Danny twirling my keys.

"Shhh!"

"The mass is ended. Go in peace to love and serve the Lord. In the name of the Father…"

"That's the wrong hand, Danny."

"Ooops! I forgot," said Danny touching every part of his body from the navel up.

"Let's go. Last one to the car is a Protestant," I said.

"What's a 'prodstint'?" asked Danny.

"Uncle Paul."

"Oh."

"Give me my keys, Danny."

"I don't have 'em."

"Don't play tricks on Daddy now. It's too hot. Give me the keys."

"I put 'em in the basket," he said hiding behind his mother.

"What?! Why did you do that?" I yelled.

"I dropped my money…I made a mistake…" The little guy was now crying.

"Ooooh! Danny's gonna get it," said Lori.

"You be quiet and sit in the car."

"Aren't you going to hit him? You always hit me," complained Lori.

"Just when it's your week," I said. "I'll be right back."

I took a quick run to the rectory and explained my problem to the priest who answered the door.

"Are you a member of Our Lady of Bunker Hill?"

"No, Father."

"I see. Well, can you describe the keys?" Could you believe it?

"Okay, guys, this is our last day in Boston so we have to move fast so we can see a lot."

"Are we gonna look at old houses again?" whined Lori.

"You bet."

"Can't we go to the pool?"

"We didn't drive 400 miles to go in a pool."

"But it's hot!"

"She's right, Tony. It's 92 already and it's only noon. Maybe we should go a little later."

"Nah, it's perfect walking weather," I said mopping my dripping brow. "I read in the guide book that there's a red line painted down the center of the sidewalk and all you have to do is follow it. It's like the *Wizard of Oz*."

"It's a *yellow* brick road in the *Wizard of Oz*," corrected Diane.

"Same thing."

"Will there be a witch?"

"No, Danny."

"Munchkins?"

"No."

"Then I don't wanna go."

"Me either."

"Me either."

"Good. Then it's all settled. Let's go."

And we went and we walked and we sweated and they complained. We went in one old house after another—me for interest, them for shade.

"Is this a church?"

"Yes. Sh!"

"But we already went to a church today."

"This is an old church." As I snapped a picture of an elaborate organ in the choir loft, a deep voice snapped at me.

"As the sign clearly states, no pictures allowed. This is a house of worship."

"My daddy said it's a *church*...and he's a teacher," said Danny.

"It figures," said the deep voice.

Because they knew we'd be in town, the entire city's Puerto Rican community was having a parade...in full garish costume. It must have been a religious festival of some kind but with the exception of the statue of the Blessed Mother, it was hard to tell. The participants were very enthusiastic, jumping over car hoods and screaming at people in Spanish. I smiled and said, "*Su madre*."

"This is the Boston Common," I announced.

"Looks like a park," said Diane.

"It is. There are boat rides over there and a big wading fountain..."

"Could we go in?"

"Sure. Take off your sneakers first."

By now it was 98...in the shade. And the fountain was gushing cool water, inviting me to throw mature caution and dignity to the wind. I waded in and got refreshingly drenched. "Come on in, Mare. It's great!"

"Are you referring to me, sir?" She always disowned me when embarrassed by my behavior.

"No, I was talking to the beautiful woman behind you."

"Do you know the car is five blocks away?"

"No, but if you hum a few bars, I'll fake it."

"That's not funny," said a little boy wading on my toes.

"Did your mother have any kids that lived?"

"That's not funny either."

"Did you hear the one about the little boy who drowned in Boston Common?"

"No," he said splashing me in the face and running away to stand on someone else's toes.

"Cute son you have there," I said to a woman who looked like she deserved him.

"He's trilingual," she said.

"I'm a teacher."

"It figures."

"Can I pee in here?" asked Danny.

"No, it's against the law."

"I already did."

We spent an uneventful last night in Boston and then set out for Marblehead and Salem. Oh I know what you're thinking. "Damn teachers always crying poor and then going off on New England vacations!" Hey! We cooked our own food on our own smuggled in electric frying pan. We had liverwurst sandwiches on the floor. We made our own lemonade. (At home we even made our own milk.) We all stayed in the same room and nobody had sex. Do you begrudge us *everything*?

Marblehead bored them and Salem scared the shit out of them.

"I didn't like that place," said Diane.

"Why not?"

"It gave me the creeps."

"Was that the *real* devil?" asked Danny.

"No," said Lori. "The *real* devil is in hell."

"Ohhh! Lori said a bad word."

"It's not a bad word if you're telling where he lives," I explained.

"The devil lives in bullshit," said Danny.

Our next stop was New Hampshire so the kids, especially Danny, could play in the sandy beaches of Hampton. It was no Atlantic City, but we managed to find a place with clean sheets. We later found out that they were spread over mattresses with curvature of the spine.

My wife was unimpressed with the beach and the countless gulls that seemed hell-bent on attacking her. She never liked any beach because she didn't like to wear a bathing suit. She claimed that her legs had too many veins and that she looked like a road map. I didn't see anything wrong with them, but then I've always liked to travel.

I thought that since we had gone this far north we might as well go all the way and take in Maine.

"We could give Mrs. Treat a call," I said. Mrs. Treat was a kindly old lady I taught with for years until her retirement. She and her widowed sister had moved to Maine two years ago and were always welcoming old friends as they passed by on their vacation jaunts.

"Oh sure. She's just *dying* to have five people drop in on her."

"She is; she likes to have people stop in. I'll call her."

"I wouldn't if I were you. What are you going to do, invite yourself?"

"I'll just tell here where we are and she'll invite us."

"Sure she will."

Well, she would have invited us if she weren't so tired. She just now got rid of a whole house full of people. And she's not as young as she used to be…and her sister minds the noise…but maybe some other time…

"I told you."

"In the profound words of Daniel Anthony Angelo—bullshit, Mare!"

We drove on to Maine anyway—just so I could say I was there. I stopped in front of a Maine Welcomes You sign and took a few pictures. Then we piled back in and headed for home.

"I have to pee."

"Of course you do."

Finally, with all the empirical evidence in, he got around to money, $700. We didn't have it, but we knew we couldn't go on corroding our intestines and our pipes as though there were no tomorrow.

"We're convinced that your products are good ones but we really can't afford anything like that just yet," said my wife. It was her standard rejection notice to all salesmen, well or ill-groomed.

"Okay. I can understand that," said the salesman. "Just let me ask you a few questions." He then proceeded to interrogate my wife unmercifully on her rate of soap consumption. "How many bars a month? boxes of laundry detergent? cleanser? dishwashing powder? shampoo? rug cleaner? floor cleaner? car soap? All right, now let me just add this all up here…Okay…If you buy the Oh So Soft Water Softener and Neutralizer tonight, we'll give you a five year supply of every kind of biodegradable soap and cleaning powder you'll need to keep your family clean and healthy."

"Five years?" repeated my wife.

"That's right, five years! And that's just to prove a point. If you were to go on using the products you now use, at the rate you use them, in five years you would have spent over $900 on laundry products alone."

"Nine hundred? No fooling?" said my wife. Numbers impressed the hell out of her. "But we still can't afford it." She didn't say *just yet* this time. That worried me.

"Tell you what. If you buy tonight, I'll throw in 3,000 S & H Green Stamps." That did it. My wife could only resist so much temptation. All this happened on a Friday night. The following Monday morning our Oh So Soft Water Softener and Neutralizer was delivered. So was our five year supply of soap and detergents.

Do you have any idea how much soap that is? Three 100 pound cardboard drums of laundry detergent; ten cases of face soap—20 bars to the case; 20 gallons of concentrated shampoo…and the list goes on and on.

That was the soap my wife was worried about, the soap that was now feeling the first ripples of torrential rains filling our basement. We ran down the steps, me in my nightshirt and Mare in her cap. "Don't just stand there," said my wife, her once fluffy bedroom slippers now looking like two drowned rats. "Move the soap to higher ground." It would probably strain my credibility if I told you that I knocked over a gallon of concentrated Oh So Soft Shampoo with Lanolin, so I won't tell you. "That's it," she said. "I'm moving!"

"Moving where?"

"To higher ground. Do you think I want to live here for the rest of my life? What about our dream house? Huh? What about it?"

"This is a nice house," I said soothingly.

"Oh sure. It's real nice. There's bats in the attic, water in the basement, and neighbors who ignore you. Yeah. It's real nice!"

"We could paint…"

"You can't paint a bat!"

"We could…"

"We could sell and move—that's what we could do!"

"See? I told you we were moving. Do I have to go to a different school?" Lori was starting to cry.

"I can't stand it here any more. I'm even afraid to go out in the yard to hang up the wash. HE is always peeping out his window at me."

HE was Horace, the crazy guy who lived next door and thought we were always talking about him. One afternoon when I returned home from the joys of academe, Crazy Horace was standing in my driveway. That in itself was peculiar because Crazy Horace only came out twice a month to mow half his lawn. In the seven years I lived next to him he never cut the grass all in one clip. Lots of times he merely mowed a swath from his door to his car.

"Hi Horace. How you doin'?"

"If your wife was a man," he growled, "I'd punch her!"

"If she was a man, I never would've married her."

"It's not funny, Angelo. I'm sick of all the talk. I heard her pumping my wife full of questions. 'Is Horace back to work? Is Horace on vacation? What's Horace doing lately? If I can help out, let me know.' I'm sick of that shit! You hear me?!" The question was rhetorical…the entire neighborhood could hear him.

"I'll tell you what, Horace. You get your ass out of my driveway before you end up with steel-belted radial tread marks on your crazy head!" And he did and I never saw or spoke to him again for two whole years. My wife and I pledged then and there that if we ever moved into our dream house, we'd check the neighborhood carefully for people who make Christianity easier.

"Has he been bothering you again, Mare? Has he said anything to you?"

"No, he just peeps!"

"Danny peeps too when I take a bath," said Lori.

"Just go brush your teeth, Lori," I said. "And close the door…Maybe you can hang the wash in the basement, Mare."

"You want your shirts to mildew?"

"Maybe…"

"Maybe nothing. I'm going to get a job and we're going to MOVE!"

Lori yelled from the bathroom with a mouth full of paste, "See? I told ya!"

"A teaching job?"

"Teaching?!" She was heating up, her red cheeks puffed out. "I wouldn't take a job teaching if they paid me. Remember when I applied as a substitute and Dowager put me on the list? Maybe you don't remember because it was two years ago! Know how many times I was called? Do you? Huh? Do you? None! That's how many! And do you know why? Because I'm your wife, that's why, Mr. Perfect. When they see *Angelo,* all they think of is you and your big mouth...and your articles...and your letters to the newspaper."

"Maybe you could change your name."

"And cut out the jokes. If I change anything, it'll be my address."

"Lori says I have to go to a different school," said Diane crying in the doorway.

My wife folded back the newspaper and said, "Here's one for a Shift Clerk at Paradise Farm."

"That's a bakery. You want to work in a bakery? God, if it's like Dorkmann's..."

"If it's like Dorkmann's what?" she interrupted. "People there not *perfect* enough for you, Mr. Teacher of the Year?"

"Don't start, Mare."

"Don't YOU start yelling. You always start yelling so the whole neighborhood knows our business."

"I'll yell if I want to yell," I yelled. "You're always telling me what to do!" I yelled even louder.

"And you always never do it," she said softly. It was a trick. Whenever she got me mad, she would lower her voice because she knew I would raise mine. Then she would shift the argument from the topic at hand to my big mouth. "Now if you're through drawing attention to yourself, I'm going to call about this job."

"Go ahead and call! See if I care. That way you'll finally be fulfilled." I walked over to the kitchen door and yelled through the screen, "My wife is going to get fulfilled! In a bakery!"

She got the job. It was a NIGHT shift clerk. And Lori was right—we were going to move.

"Did you send in the ad, Mr. I'm So Good With Words I Don't Need A Realtor?" she asked.

"Yup."

"Is it any good?' she asked.

"It's a beaut," I answered. "Wait'll you see it."

If you know anybody that wants to buy a charming four-bedroom Cape Cod with an indoor pool on a busy street across from a huge apartment complex, let me know. Call Alfie at 555-275-7823.

She started work on a Sunday. She neglected to tell me that she'd have to work on Sundays and holidays and every other day except Saturdays. "Well, it's time," she said nervously. "Now make sure the kids are in bed by nine. School tomorrow, you know. And Danny needs a bath...And you can heat up that lasagna for supper...How do I look?"

"You look great." She always looked great. People would never guess that she lived in a twenty-year old Cape Cod. "Good luck." I kissed her and then was pushed out of the way so the kids could kiss her too.

"Bye, Mom. I love you," said Lori.

"Bye, Mom. I love you," said Diane.

"Me too," said Danny. "Where you goin'?"

"Mommy's going to work. Now you be a good boy for Daddy." I thought she was going to cry.

"I'll wait up for you."

"You don't have to. I won't be home until 12:30 and you have to get up early."

"I want to." Then *she* kissed *me*. It was all very touching. You would think that we'd never see each other again.

"Are we going to move?" asked Diane.

"Who told you that?"

"Lori. She said we're going to move. Are we?"

"Lori has big ears."

"I know but are we going to move?" persisted Diane.

"We'll see," I said, already assuming my wife's persona.

At six I fed the kids lasagna. They didn't eat much...mainly because I set the oven for pre-heat. "What's all this black stuff on top?" asked Lori holding her nose.

"Mozzarella."

"How come it's black?"

"Scrape it off."

"Bleech!" said Diane.

"I'm not eating this even if there is dessert." Lori was way ahead of me.

"If you don't, don't tell me later that you're hungry." Good God! My wife always says *that* too.

soon after. My friend Carmen and I gave her an elaborate funeral. Carmen said High Mass in Latin. Well, maybe not Latin but something that sounded foreign and Church-like. We blessed ourselves and genuflected and sang *Ave Maria*. Carmen had a beautiful voice and an uncanny ear for pretend-Latin. The cat was nameless, even though Borzoni had her for years. Carmen said we should call her *Puta*. So we did.

Carmen wanted to bury the litter with her, but I explained that they were not yet dead. Carmen could sing and say mass, but he was not the brightest candle on the altar.

This was not a good neighborhood for pets. If animals could fend for themselves they were welcome. Dave, Lucky, and Carmelooch were the exception, not the rule. I learned that the hard way.

Borzoni bought me chicks for Easter when I was about six or seven years old. They were pink and purple and green, small enough to fit into the palm of my little kid hand. I was beside myself with joy. The chicks...I called them Peeps...were for me. Given to me by Borzoni, a man who never gave anybody anything. I fed them, I watered them, I named them. I took loving care of them as they shed their colors and became white and brown chickens. They clucked when I came near and even ate out of my hands. I thought they were pets. I found out one Labor Day that they were dinner.

Pat Conroy wrote about the mistreatment of animals in his book *The Water Is Wide*. He blamed the Yamacraw Island kids' behavior on their isolation from "mainland civilization." I'm of the opinion that all kids live on islands isolated from common sense and decency. They are an evil lot on a daily search for something they can control. It was Biblical. The Lord God said: "It is not good for kids to be alone." So the Lord God formed out of the ground various wild animals and various birds of the air, and He brought them to the kids to be abused.

We caught fireflies...called lightning bugs where I came from. The meek among us put them in Mason jars and released them the next morning. Kids like Carmen would make rings of them by crushing their flashing bodies around their middle fingers. We thought that was a brave move because we all knew that lightning bugs caused warts.

Oh and you never bought a lime Hokey Pokey—that's a Snow Cone—from that little old guy with the ice wagon because some kid died after eating one.

Carmen made *streamers* of the bugs on the Fourth of July. He'd deftly snatch them from the hot and humid summer air and dash them to the ground. Then he'd quickly slide one of his black clodhoppers toward him and...*Voila!* glowing streamers of squashed lightning bugs.

Carmen could catch flies too. He said he was *training* them. And because they were resistant, he would tear out their wings. Sometimes just one wing so he could watch them squirm around in circles. "See? They're trained." And he'd flash that big goofy smile of his while he slowly amputated one leg after the other. He even did that to a praying mantis once. And that, we all knew, was illegal in the state of Pennsylvania. Chi Chi Bondi threatened to tell on him. Carmen threatened to beat her up. And Carmen didn't threaten idly.

Some lazy summer days I'd sit under an oozing peach tree and watch the ants go about their business. They'd march in single file and go up and down the tree carrying bits of leaves or other ants...dead ones, I guessed. Carmen joined me one day. "Whatcha doin'?"

"Watching the ants," I said as my gaze followed the marching column to a two-inch mound the army had created at the base of the tree.

"Watch this," said Carmen as he flattened the hill. In minutes those that were not crushed began the business of rebuilding. Carmen gave them two minutes then repeated the crushing process. "Dumb ass ants!" There was that smile again.

There were no pets more exotic than cats and dogs. Although there were rumors that Felix up the street had a snake. Carmen said he'd like to see it because he heard that if you cut off a snake's head another would grow back. Carmen was the kind of kid who'd grow up to be an ax-murderer...or a Republican senator.

Kids and adults on my street treated dogs like dogs. No canned food. No puppy biscuits. No fancy collars...flea or otherwise. The dogs ate what we ate...if there was anything left. And they slept outside, even in the winter. If they wandered off, they became somebody else's problem. I had a dog. I called him Chips. He was part Collie and part horse's ass. He did nothing but bark and Borzoni did nothing but beat him. I'm sure that's why he ran away.

"Nun jew cry for that bastard," said Borzoni. "He barka too much."

"He's a DOG," I said in Chips' defense.

"He's a bastard!" said Borzoni.

"Ma, I won a turkey."

"*Che?*"

"A turkey. I won a turkey at the dance."

"Atsa nice, En-doe-knee. Go putta in the Frigidaire."

All the ladies in my neighborhood called their refrigerators Frigidaire, the tissues Kleenex, and their soda Coca Cola. They had brand name loyalty but they bought whatever was on sale. The Coke in my house was usually Frank's Black Cherry Wishnik. "Is it Frank's? Thanks." That's what all the kids said. I never knew what Wishnik was and I'm not sure I'm spelling it right. But it was red and bubbly and cold. That's all a kid has to know.

"Are you sure?"

"*Che patzo*! Sure ahma sure. *Andiamo*. Hurry up."

The door prize at the high school holiday dance was a turkey...a LIVE turkey with a big red bow tied around its scrawny neck and attached to a leash. I pulled my prize into the *palor*.

"*Jesu Cristo mio*! Atsa no dead!" The turkey was in attack mode and my mother was the target. "*Jesu*! Ged him outta here!"

My grandfather told me to put him in the shed out back and not to get too friendly with him. "We gonna eat that bastard on Thanksgive. Nun jew give him no name. *Capische*?" I was in the ninth grade now and Borzoni thought I was ripe for a rite of passage. "YOU gonna kill that bastard...next week." I didn't think I could do it. Not alone anyway. Who could I get to help?

"Whatcha doin?" Carmen's usual greeting.

"Feeding the turkey. He's gonna be our Thanksgiving dinner."

"Who's gonna kill him?"

"Me."

"For real? All by yourself?"

"Wanna help?" Carmen's goofy smile started to drip drool.

"For real?" He was breathing heavy.

"Know how to do it?"

"Sure I do. Who don't know how to kill a turkey? You just chop off its head, dumbass."

The day of doom arrived. So did Carmen. He came early. In fact he came to my house every day the entire week asking, "Do we bump him off today, Ant? Huh? Do we?"

"My grandfather says to use the hatchet."

"No shit. Who don't know that?"

"He said one should hold him while the other chops." Carmen reached for the hatchet. A funny look crossed his eyes as he ran his thumb gently across the blade.

"Okay, Ant. Grab his legs and hold him still."

The turkey sensed that something was afoot. It hopped out of my grasp and ran gobbling around the shed. I chased it into a corner while it flapped its big wings at me. It was poised for attack. So was Carmen.

"We can't kill him in here. My grandfather will kick my ass."

"Let's jump on him. The two of us. He won't know what hit him." And so we did…kicking and cursing, gobbling and flapping. We carried him outside. The turkey was not going gently into his last night. We put him on the back step. Carmen raised the hatchet.

"What the hell are you doing?! You wanna kill me?!" I was now the only one holding the frenzied bird.

"Hold his neck down," said Carmen, "and keep your hands out of the way." He was going to do it. He was really going to do it. I couldn't look. I heard the swoosh of the hatchet zip past my ear, then a muffled sound of impact. I closed my eyes tight when I felt a spray of blood. I couldn't hold on any longer. I let him go and to my shock he took off. He started running around the yard, his head hanging on by a thread and bobbing from side to side. "He's not dead!"

"No shit, Dick Tracy! Why'd you let him go?" Carmen was frothing as he dove for the bird, hatchet raised, eyes burning with blood lust. "Grab him so I can let him have another." I did and he did but it was not in the same spot. The turkey lived on, its beak dragging along the ground as it tried to escape Carmen's wrath. "Three strikes and you're out, you bastard!" He sounded just like my grandfather. He whacked him again…the *coup de foie gras!* The bird gave up the ghost. It was time to turn him over to my mother who was waiting by the boiling pot in the kitchen.

"Nice-ah job, Carmenooch. Stick'em inna da pot. Nun jew splash." Carmen held my mutilated door prize by its feet and dunked the poor bastard into the boiling water.

"Atsa 'nough. Take 'em out." And then my mother became Carmen, attacking the feathers with abandon, pulling and plucking, alternately praising and damning saints. "*Che bruto*," she said when all the feathers were gone revealing a black and blue turkey breast. She looked at Carmen. He looked back, beaming with shy pride.

I went petless for years until I married and bought my wife her dream house, a prerequisite for dog ownership. He was a white Samoyed-German Shepherd mix. His name was Fred. I went to the local branch of the S.P.C.A.—I let it be known in the neighborhood that it was for humanitarian, not monetary reasons. I was going to *adopt* a poor hapless creature and give it a loving home where three little kids could take turns tormenting it. And somehow the S.P.C.A. knew.

"I'm sorry but you can't adopt if you have children under five. And you certainly can't adopt over the Christmas holidays. It's much too traumatic for the adoptee." The lady never once used the word *dog*. "Come back some other time."

"What'll happen to that little white puppy in number three?"

"If he's not adopted in two weeks he'll be put to sleep." She was chillingly casual about it. "I'm sorry, but we have our rules." (I swear she was a moonlighting teacher.)

"My son'll be five in two weeks."

"Tell him happy birthday," she said moving on to the next batch of adoptive parents.

I returned after a long two weeks to find that Fred was still there, wagging his tail to beat the band. The lady let me pick him up. He licked my face and peed on my shirt. I still brought him home.

He was a cute little puppy that overnight grew into a strong, leg-humping clump of shedding fur. "You better get that dog fixed before I get YOU fixed." My wife was not an animal lover.

"Is he broke?" My son Danny took everything literally.

I took him to the vet who screwed me out of $125 and saw to it that Fred would never screw anybody out of anything. When I brought him home he was still groggy from the operation. He barely moved. "Now THAT'S a good dog," said my wife.

The next day things were back to normal. Fred was out front mounting the mailbox.

My kids loved to play with him but they hated to feed, walk, or brush him. "Don't look at me," said my wife. "You wanted a dog. You have a dog. Enjoy him, Mister Man's Best Friend. Just keep him off my new rug." It was a gold oval made special to lie in front of our fireplace. It had gold tassels all around. Fred was not allowed on it. He was allowed *AROUND* it but not on it. He became a tightrope walker as he maneuvered his white shedding bulk around the fringes. The side closest to the fireplace only afforded about three inches of rugless flooring and was therefore the most challenging. Fred was up for it. Or at least he thought he was. Three-fourths of the way around he'd lose his balance and keel over. He was fun to watch and my kids often called him into the family room just to see him fall. He died thirteen years later. He lasted five more years than the rug.

I had him cremated, his ashes resting in a gold coffee can on my filing cabinet. Once a year I shake him.

AMNESTY DAY

I loved teaching ninth grade kids. But then the higher ups found out, transformed the system, and sent me to the new middle school. Ha! Ha! I loved that too. It took a lot more energy and it was obvious that God was not done with those kids, but I loved it. They found out again and transferred me to the high school. Turns out that that's where I probably belonged all along. I never had so much fun in all my professional life. All those crazy kids who climbed walls and frayed nerves years before had turned into human beings that you could actually talk to. Some even let you teach them something.

The Facade Area School District decided to do away with the "Basic" designation for its 11th and 12th grade English classes. It was felt that the appellation was demeaning and did little to raise self-esteem. What was demeaning were all the baby books and worksheets that beat the Basics into submission. Either that or they dropped out. It was felt that calling them Academic would motivate them, challenge them to new heights, make scholars of them. Notice all the *FELT* stuff. Nothing about "research shows"…Facade was just into feelings. And so the kids became academic. They couldn't read any better and they couldn't write without a translator, but boy did they feel good about themselves. And why shouldn't they? They were all passing, many earning A's and B's. And of course they were all going to college. Their counselors said so.

By now I knew how to play the game. I relied on Br'er Rabbit for inspiration. "Okay. I'll teach in the high school. Just don't give me those academic kids. I want to teach Shakespeare and literary analysis and rhetoric." When I got my schedule for the year it was loaded with academic classes starting with the very first period. Little did they know how suited I was for the briar patch.

We got along fine…me and the kids. I made them write every day. I made them talk every day. And we made each other laugh every day. Long about Christmas time…in those days you still could say Christmas without getting into trouble…I greeted the class with my usual obnoxiously loud "Good morning" which I repeated ad nauseum until I got an equally loud if not enthusiastic reply. "Today," I said, "is Amnesty Day." With a flourish I wrote the words on the board…which were still black in those days…and turned to the class. "Who knows what that means? Akbar?" Akbar never knew the answers to anything but I liked the sound of his name and called on him often.

"It's not even 8 o'clock yet," said Akbar pointing to the wall clock. He wasn't being rude or insolent. He was just being tired. They all were. It was just too early for high school seniors.

"Anybody know? Come on. Think. Amnesty Day." I was pleading and Monte could sense it. He was a good kid who always volunteered the wrong answers with conviction and a smile.

"It means you can't have sex today," said he with a wall-to-wall grin.

"No, you asshole," said the kid behind him. "That's abstinence." Wow! That kid was a REAL academic. I didn't want to lose him, but I also didn't want his epithet to go uncorrected. I turned to the board again and wrote EUPHEMISM in big bold letters.

"Anybody know what *that* means?" I ignored Monte's raised arm. This was a teachable moment and I was not going to let it pass. I shared Greek etymology of the word and how it came to mean using less distasteful words to make a point. I turned to the board again and wrote SHIT. *Shit* always got their attention. I had used it before in a grammar review of parts of speech. We learned that there was a great variety in shit…from noun to verb to adjective to interjection and then back again. "You can't say *shit* in school so you come up with substitutes, right?" They knew the drill from here on. The Class Secretary rose and pried the chalk from my yellow-coated fingers. She had the neatest, nicest handwriting and was selected by the class to write the notes on the board because my handwriting was just too sloppy to decipher. I claimed arthritis; they claimed old age.

"Shoot."

"Crap."

"Stuff."

"Poop."

"Turd."

It was no different back in the days of Catholic school. Carmen, the Turkey Slayer and life-long member of the Buzzard reading group, was hopeless. Today he'd be the poster child for learning support entitled to 250 accommodations. He could never get the required prayers quite right, a shortcoming Sister reminded him daily that would lead to eternal damnation. Carmen's rendition of the Lord's Prayer: "Our Father, warts in heaven, Harold be thy name…mumble, mumble, mumble…lead us not into Penn's station…"

"No! No! No!" Sister would scream. And Carmen would try again usually making it worse. It would go on until he cried.

He wasn't any better with the Hail Marys. He insisted it was "blessed is thy *room* Jesus" or sometimes offering Sister "thy *wound* Jesus." She would have none of it.

"No! No! No! It's 'womb! Womb! WOMB!'" she would bellow.

"What's a womb," asked Carmen in all innocence.

Sister never said.

Carmen had the voice of an angel and loved when we had music lessons. They weren't lessons really. We'd just sing holy songs whenever the Holy Ghost moved Sister. (He didn't become *Spirit* till much later.) While we sang "bringing in the sheaves," at the top of his lungs Carmen sang "bringing in the sheep." Even when we had art lessons…that's when Sister was in a good mood and let us draw with the unbroken crayons…Carmen could find a way to screw it up. One time we listened to the story of the first Christmas and were told to draw the manger scene. Carmen drew a half decent picture of Mary holding the baby Jesus. He also drew a fat guy and stuck him in the corner next to a cow.

"Carmen, who is that?" asked Sister.

As always the malapropistic artist beamed with shy pride. "Like in the song, 'ster. Round John Virgin, Mother and Child."

As Art Linkletter used to say, "Kids say the darndest things." Every teacher knows that to be true. Just when you think you heard them all, a new one comes along. Those you hear first period you forget before you get a chance to share them in the faculty room at the end of the day. But when they write them down, they are preserved forever. I'll bet every teacher has a drawer full of kid screw-ups.

My biggest collection is kids' excuses. For forty years I amassed sometimes hilarious sometimes pathetic reasons why kids didn't do their homework. Understand that I took it personally if kids didn't do their assignments. I told them I was insulted and that I deserved an explanation. My teachers *next store* and across the hall would scream and carry on as though they were servants of the Immaculate Heart of Mary whenever their students didn't come across with homework.

And when they were done all their yelling, they'd give the kids zeros. What I did was give the kids another chance.

"I don't have mine, Mr. Angelo. But I can give it to you on Monday."

"Well then, Michael, you'll have to write The Management (that's what I called myself for 40 years) a letter explaining the extenuating circumstances surrounding your late submission." When Michael said "HUH?" I launched into a vocabulary lesson on the meaning of *extenuating circumstances* and the human need to be given a second chance. I told the kids that we all forget or have personal problems…they call them *issues* today…that get in the way of what school requires.

"Do I still get a zero if I write the letter?"

"No, Michael. Just attach your letter to the paper you owe. If your letter is convincing enough, I'll read and grade your essay without penalty. If it stinks (today they would say if it sucks), I'll return to sender. Oh, and I expect that it will LOOK like a letter and that it be placed in a properly addressed envelope and hand delivered to my mailbox."

"You mean at your house?"

"Of course at my house. And for your information I take my wife on a movie date every Saturday. We both like Hershey bars…with almonds." Thus began a four-decades long collection of not only excuses and candy but also my other obsession…chocolate-chip cookies.

See? No yelling. No embarrassment. I just dumped it back on the kids…prompting many of them to call themselves The Managed. Nine out of ten kids used this OUT just once. The recidivists, however, were like the poor: they will always be with us.

From my archives…
December 16, 1986

Dear Mr. Angelo,

Before you think about my late paper, think about this. Warm, moist chocolate chip cookies melting in your mouth, the smell of each delicious confection wafting and lingering around your olfactory senses. Each chestnut brown chip caught between your teeth. Think of a favor for a favor—an unforgettable sensation in exchange for what? a mere acceptance of a late paper. When measured, the odds are greatly in your favor.

I am deeply sorry for turning in my vocabulary assignment late. Preparations for the holiday season such as: shopping, wrapping presents, BAKING...kept me busy.

My sincere apologies,
Rachel P.

ps My lunch table helped me write this!

Shortly after that one reached my mailbox, this one showed up:

Dear Mr. Angelo,

This paper is late because my creative talents were so focused on helping my dear friend Rachel P. write an original letter to get HER late papers excused that I didn't have time to do my own work. In this world of selfishness and materialism, I like to help my fellow man and put his own needs before mine whenever possible.

Sincerely yours,
Lisa K.

March 2, 1987
Dear Mr. Angelo,

It's me again, and I promise I will bring you another batch of cookies if you except (sic) this paper late. If you would like a description of these delicious chocolate chip cookies, please refer to the last late excuse letter. Thank you for your time,

The Chocolate chip expert,
Rachel

To: The Management
From: Doris T.

Re: Late work
Date: 12.16.98

You are the best teacher in this school. Please accept this late work and don't take off a lot of points. This is my first time turning work in late; I usually turn it in early.

(I couldn't find one with almonds. I hope this is just as good.)

ps
You were looking good today.

Doris did indeed submit assignments early. And every time she did I gave her ten extra credit points. And, yes, I was most susceptible to flattery…that and a milk chocolate Hershey bar.

Dear Sir;

On March 16 a vocabulary assignment was due. On March 15 I forgot all about it, and therefore did not do the above-mentioned assignment. I am not lying, I swear.

Through the goodness of your heart I hope you will accept this assignment on March 17. It would be reasonable to accept it because it is my first and, hopefully, last offense. And also because I did not mention your receding hairline.

I hope that one day this letter will be printed in the book you say you're going to publish. If it isn't, then I'll have to rip off your back pocket.

I'm not lying,
Mike

Oh yeah? Well, here it is, Mike. I didn't even cut out that stupid-ass line about my back pocket.

Dearest Mr. Angelo,

Before I get to the reason of this letter please allow me to say you are looking trimmer and younger with every day that goes by. You work out, don't you? So do I, as you can most likely tell. Anyway, due to a slight mental lapse that bestowed itself upon me Thursday night, I forgot about the short story assignment that was due. Perhaps it was the diligent work I was doing on my autobiography, or it may have been my enthrallment with the latest novel I am reading that caused me to fail to remember such a vital assignment. I am aware of the fact that I probably deserve a zero on account of my stupidity, but I am also aware that you are a kind, forgiving man with a big heart and that you could surely overlook this one blunder. I respectfully remind you of my pristine record of punctuality on all of my assignments to this point, and guarantee you that this is the first and last time you will be put into this position. Sir, my future rests in your hands. I am confident that you will rule prudently, and fairly.

Mercifully,
Kevin C.

Mr. Angelo,

Please excuse the lateness of the two short story analyses that I turned in yesterday. The reasons they were late are:

1. I have had many problems in my personal life,

2. I am at times prone to do poorly on out of class assignments...

Those reasons compounded with the fact I need the points should persuade you, the all-powerful teacher, to have mercy on such a pitiful little honors student like myself. I am throwing myself on the mercy of your kindness. Please accept my work so that I can get good grades and become a better student to fulfill your dreams of me going to college.

Sincerely,
John B.

ps
Did I mention that I worship the ground you walk on?

Dear Mr. Angelo,

This letter is regarding my vocabulary assignments. I failed to turn them in on the date they were due. The reason being that I was very absent-minded and forgot to bring home my English notebook. I'm usually not this forgetful, but I guess I had a lot on my mind.

I know I haven't been keeping up with my homework like I should, and I hope to improve on this starting now.

I hope you can understand. I know it is probably very annoying to have work turned in late.

Thank you.
Christine D.

Smart kid, that Christine. She anticipated the opposition. She said it before I could. Of course I accepted her work late.

"Tony, you are such a pushover! That kid is playing you like a mandolin."

"Mandolin? What do you mean 'playing me like a mandolin?'"

"Mandolin is Italian."

"So?"

"So...*you're* Italian."

"That's not funny."

"Yeah well...you're still a pushover."

"Yeah well, you're still a pain in the ass."

Ah! Another meaningful conversation between colleagues advancing the cause of public education and the vagaries of tardy adolescents!

Greetings:

This is a letter informing you of my late homework that was due on March 2nd but was not turned in by this hard-working student on the required date.

I hope you can understand my situation and accept my late paper. I know what an understanding and well-liked man you are. I know you wouldn't want to ruin such a well-earned reputation.

Thanks so much!
Your good student,
Carol W.

"Not another one! How many times are you going to fall for that crap? She's just trying to flatter you, you know?"

"You're right. I wish I were more like you. You can see right through that crap. I guess the kids can't pull the silk over **your** eyes."

"Indeed they can't. And it's *wool*, not silk."
"Hey, what do you expect from a mandolin?"

Remember Decius in *Julius Caesar*?
  Said he,

  "...unicorns may be betrayed with trees
  and bears with glasses, elephants with holes,
  Lions with toils, and men with flatterers:
  But when I tell him [Caesar] he hates flatterers,
  He says he does, being then most flattered."

I could never see anything wrong with accepting nice remarks at face value:

  "I know your kind nature will allow you to understand my position."

  "You're the best English teacher I've had in my whole life."

Even this one:
  "Everything the kids say about you is true."

When you collect over one hundred and fifty essays a week, you are not thrown off kilter because some harried kid turned one in on Monday instead of Friday. Of course my colleagues thought otherwise.
  "What are you teaching that kid? That he can turn things in whenever he wants? He won't be able to get away with that in the REAL world. You're doing him a disservice."
  "What do you suggest?"
  "Take points off. That's the *least* you could do."
  "Is that what *you* do?" I already knew the answer. My colleague *next store* had a much-deserved reputation of being a prick when it came to late work. In his long tenure he was able to come up with a complicated formula of point deductions that only he could fathom.
  "Of *course* that's what I do. I knock off thirty-three points per day of lateness."
  "Why thirty-three?"
  "It's more than twenty-five and less than fifty." He looked at me over his glasses as if to say, "What ass doesn't know that?!"
  "Hey, I'm just a mandolin."
  "Huh?"
  "Never mind."

But I did think about what he said. What *was* I teaching the kid if I let him turn stuff in late? I wondered if they ever asked Bundy or Gacy or Hitler if they ever got away with turning in something late. First an essay, then a term paper, then Poland and France. Yikes!

Dear Mr. Angelo,

I am handing in my short story summary today instead of yesterday because I could not get it completed. If I had rushed and written it fast, it would not have met your writing approval. I realize that I had all weekend to write it, but I had to deal with some very confusing and upsetting events in my life. I am deeply sorry and hope that you will accept my late paper without penalization.

Sincerely,
Karen L.

ps
You probably don't want to hear this, but...this is my first offense!

Mr. Angelo,

This assignment is late because I procrastinated doing it, then I just never did it.

From,
Jessica C.

Dear to Whom it may concern:

I'm just asking for your sympathy this one time, and it will never happen again.

Sincerely yours,
Raymond C.

How could you not accept this one?

> This past weekend I had the unfortunate pleasure of experiencing the nasty repercussions of an intestinal virus. Consequently, the majority of my time was spent remedying this. In the future, I hope that I'll never have to experience a weekend like that ever again.

Or this one?

> There is actually no excuse for my lateness. I hope this will not cause you to renounce any previous impressions you had about me.

Or this from a kid who was clever enough to shove in twelve of the vocabulary words under study the week he came up short with his homework. Can you spot them?

> Dear Mr. Angelo,
>
> Over the course of my life I have become adept at making plausible excuses. Recently I have learned that I am not beguiling anyone. I made a mistake and can only ask for absolution. While I have no stories of apocalypse in my homework folder, there were two events preceding Friday which augmented my forgetfulness. On Wednesday I was sick and after circumambulating my room, promptly fell asleep after school. I awoke half an hour later to eat dinner in the evening and fell asleep again. On Thursday I exacerbated the situation by leaving my books in school before the golf team left for its match all day. We returned after school was over. While these do not justify my insufferable mistake, I thought you should know about them. I assure you that this will not happen again during this millennium. Can you find it in your altruistic heart to give me benediction and accept this late paper?
>
> Josh

Dear Sir,

The reason for my lateness is quite good. I asked my neighbor if I could borrow his VCR recording of the Death of a Salesman. He lent it over this past weekend and gave me more insite of the character Dustin Hoffman. I think it helped me write a better paper. I hope you do to.

Sincerely,
Bob McC

Dear Mr. Angelo:

I am writing to you to discuss the due date of the rough draft of our English term paper. It would make life so much easier if you would postpone the due date until May 5.

There are several extenuating circumstances regarding this request. The first and most important concerns the SAT's. I am taking this test on Saturday. Since this test makes a huge difference concerning what colleges will be willing to accept me, I would like to prepare for it. A friend of ours is fortunate enough to own a computer program that helps you prepare for it. Recently he told me that he would be more than happy to let me use it this week. The only available time for me is tonight since I worked last night and have to work Wednesday and Thursday nights. It would be extremely difficult for me to finish my term paper and go over to my mother's friend's house and work on the computer all in one night. If I had the weekend to put on the finishing touches I would be able to write a college-bound paper. The reason I want to extend the date until Monday is because I have an entire Spanish term paper due Friday and sections of my history term paper due the same day.

If you could find it in your heart to postpone this due date it would make my life much easier.

Sincerely,
Rob W.

The teachers at the Fire and Brimstone Lunch Table would have ripped this kid a new asshole. You could put some hard-earned cash on any one of these reactions:

1.   They would read the kid's letter aloud to the entire class…whining the words as though they were on the verge of tears.

2.   They would give the kid a lecture on time management.

3.   They would castigate the kid's sense of priorities. How dare he place Spanish or history or even SAT's before English class!

4.   They would make an overhead projection of the letter calling attention to all the spelling and punctuation errors.

5.   They would do all of the above…and then give the kid a zero.

Mr. Angelo:

Mr. Angelo, I forgot to do it two days ago so I did it in study hall yesterday. But I didn't get it totally completed so I decided to get it finished and turn it in late.

Sincerely,
Corbett

Note:

Corbett never did say what *it* was. To this day I don't have a clue. I am, however, still willing to accept it.

Dear Sir:

I am writing this letter regarding the Short Story Summary that I didn't turn in on Monday. Well, I couldn't find it.

I, being a college bound student, had finished the assignment early, but I just had trouble keeping track of it. On Monday, it was nowhere to be seen. Today I found it in my History folder. Lord only knows why it was there!

Sorry for the inconvenience.

Sincerely,
Kimberly P.

To: Mr. Angelo
From: Candice c.
Re: Ch. 4 Vocab is late
Date: 12/18

I apologize for my tardiness. My word processor has ceased to exist.

Here's a letter that knocked my socks off and crossed my eyes:

Dear Mr. Angelo,

I am writing to you regarding the late paper that I hope to receive credit for. As I see it, pleading with you is probably not the most judicious strategy, so instead I hope to persuade you that, by accepting my late paper, you will yourself benefit in many ways. Your karma will improve, your power as a teacher will be augmented, and the rumor that you are the best teacher at Facade High School will be justified once again, thus further solidifying your chances of eventually establishing an insuperable and widespread dictatorship over students and faculty alike.

What goes around comes around. As I said, accepting late papers can only improve your standing in life's cosmic scheme.

And then he threw in some stuff which I took as Catholic doctrine—

I think the point is clear--whatever you have been searching for or wanting recently, you will receive seven of them as gifts within a week of accepting my late paper.

St. Anthony, right?

There are less noble reasons to do this, however. Imbedded in the human psyche is the concept of reimbursement. When you do something nice for someone else, you are simultaneously getting something in return. And it isn't as abstract as good karma. What you are getting is an unspoken but unbreakable promise from the beneficiary of your benevolence. If you accept my late paper, I automatically owe you something in return. That something is left up to you. And if I were in your shoes, I would think long and hard about it. After all, no one knows where I'll be in ten years. The idea is that, by doing favors for others, you are quite literally accumulating power that you can utilize later on.

He couldn't stop writing and I couldn't stop reading. Could you?

But by far the most exciting reason to do something unnecessarily kind is that it will enhance your reputation. It is a quotidian observation that you are probably the best teacher at Facade. But why stop there? Through magnanimity you could eventually become renowned as the best teacher in the district. Before long, you could be the best in the state. The only two remaining strata are the country and the world. And your power will rise with your prominence, albeit more slowly. As more students, parents, and coworkers grow to like and even love you, the number of your supporters will proliferate. The more supporters you reel in, the more influence you will have in school-related matters.

Here comes the schmooze...

Accepting my late paper would be the first step; after that, everything else would fall into place. Gradually, you would rise to a position commensurate with that of Caesar or Napoleon. The common people (the students, I suppose) would treat your words as gospel, would look to you with admiration and even awe, would possibly even applaud when you entered the room. Why would you let a future like this slip from your grasp?

Why indeed!?

At this point, there are really only two possibilities. Either you are convinced or you aren't. If the latter is true, then I have no choice but to resort to begging. Please accept my late paper. I know that "I forgot" isn't an excuse; it's simply the truth, plain and simple. I emphatically stress that my forgetfulness does NOT reflect on my estimation of your class...

And now the clincher...

...on the contrary, I look forward to every lesson and even enjoy completing English assignments. I am just a forgetful person. I have forgotten my own mother's birthday many times. I don't think I've ever remembered my father's birthday. It doesn't mean I don't love them. Neither does my forgetfulness regarding the short story analysis mean that I don't care about English. Really, all it means is that I was too foolish to write that particular assignment in my aptly named assignment book.

Sincerely,
Daniel T.

Sometimes an *entire class* would write. Like this one:

Mr. Anthony A. Angelo
c/o Facade High School
re: term paper

We, your third period English class, are in a terrible position. We have all been struggling over our term paper due Friday, April twenty-fifth, and just can't seem to find the right resources and put it together correctly.

Considering the fact that we are all responsible young adults we promise to have the rough draft in on Monday, if your heart will allow it. After spending almost an entire school year with you, we have come to know you as a caring, understanding, warm, kind, sensitive, handsome man and know that you understand our awful situation.

Please, Mr. Angelo, we would certainly appreciate this weekend to work like diligent students on our term papers.

Bless your soul.

Your humble servants.
Third Period English

I granted their request. I looked at it this way. Here was going to be a weekend free of papers, and 35 kids were going to be kept off the streets. It was actually a community service. And it wasn't even *my* idea. A *kid* came up with it…a kid usually comes up with *all* the good stuff.

This kid Elyse was right on.

Dear Mr. Angelo:

I am a student in one of your English classes. May I just say that I love and admire the way you and your staff enthusiastically teach. (She viewed my student teacher as staff.) I enjoy being in your bright and colorful class. However, there is one minor suggestion that I would like to make.

You see, my English class is an abnormally large class consisting of at least thirty or so students. I was simply wondering if you might find it insightful to lessen the amount of homework that you give out each day? I, as well as many others, am extremely busy when the school day is done. I play after school sports, go to work, and in my spare time volunteer to do community service. The way I figure it, you have about six classes with maybe twenty students a day. That's almost one hundred and twenty papers of homework to grade each night. If you decrease the amount of homework you give out, your wonderful and intrigued students will have more time to write very well written papers. We will be more focused in class, have more time to do stuff like study, and won't limit ourselves to writing incomplete papers.

You on the other hand would have more time to grade our papers and read them more thoroughly. Another big plus is that you would have more free time to yourself! If students don't like taking home tons of work, I'm sure you don't either.

So why don't you give this some thought and alleviate the pressure of having papers graded on time. Give yourself a break! A hard working teacher like yourself deserves it.

Thanks for your time.

Sincerely,
Elyse S.

My mailbox bulged with her letter and an entire *box* of Hershey bars...with almonds.

"You mean you tell the kids where you live?" My colleagues were incredulous. "You want to get your house egged?"

I had never thought about that although one of my neighbors must have. One Mischief Night he put out a big sign on his lawn that said:

The Teacher Lives Over There...with a great big arrow pointing to my house.

The kids did pull pranks once in a while but never anything destructive. In fact they did funny stuff. For instance, one early Sunday morning I went outside to pick up the paper. It was on my lawn...as were over 25 **For Sale** signs from a variety of realtors. They were arranged in cemetery rows. The effect was quite humorous.

Another time there was a toilet in the center of my yard with a LIFT sign on the seat. Of course I lifted. The underside said 'Hi Tony.' Another time my wife and I were quietly watching TV in the family room when I saw flashing lights outside our front window. Then I heard "Tony Angelo! We know you are in there. Your house is surrounded! Come out with your hands up!" The neighbors heard it too because the kids were using a bullhorn. And they all came out to watch me surrender.

Once four kids showed up on my front porch with a movie camera and as I opened the door one said: "Good evening. We are here at the beautiful home of Tony Angelo to spend Christmas with Tony and his lovely family." And they came right in. No shit! The kid with the camera went room to room before I knew what was going on. They brought a tub of Kentucky Fried Chicken and a liter of Dr. Pepper for dinner so my wife set the dining room table and we ate. After dinner one kid played Christmas tunes on the piano and we sang carols. It was a nice night.

The next day the cameraman showed his video to his classmates. One scene in particular brought the house down. "Boxers or briefs?" asked the off camera voice. "Now the truth revealed!" Zoom in to my clothes dryer. Watch the lid open. See a hand reach in and pull out my Jockey shorts. Cut to Tony singing "Don we now our gay apparel…"

The End

I have always believed that you should give back. Good or bad, you should give back…if not for posterity, then at least for revenge. I volunteered for all the committees that came down the pike. I was on Class Size Committees, Curriculum Writing Committees, Sensitivity Training Committees, Middle States Evaluating Committees, Textbook Selection Committees, Search for Superintendents Committees, Meet the School Board Candidates Committees, Graduation Ceremony Committees…and on and on.

That's why I always volunteered to take on a student teacher. Most of the ones I got were good. I even recommended them for a job. Some even for a job in the same school. A few became colleagues worthy of pride and admiration. One, Nick D'Angelo, was the absolute best. He was my clone, a joy to watch. He loved kids and they loved him.

Because our names were so much alike, kids used them interchangeably. Nick went along with it telling the kids that I was his father. Many believed him. One smart ass said I looked more like his *grand*father.

Nick was a fast learner. Show him once and he'd show you *up* the next time. He was good-looking, impeccably groomed, well-read, and reverentially polite to old guys like me. I enjoyed teasing him, but I didn't let anybody else. Eventually, like Gary, he ended up breaking my heart too. He became an administrator. I recommended him for that job almost gagging as I wrote the letter because I didn't want him to leave the classroom.

"Nick, remember what I told you."

"Yeah, I know. 'Don't forget what it was like in the classroom.' Don't worry, Tone, I won't."

The day he left, I found the nicest letter in my mailbox, a letter that made me laugh and cry. I think a part of me was in him. That's why he was the only principal I'd defend to the death. And he was the only one that didn't have a paper asshole. Nobody talked trash about Nick in my presence. Funny thing though, after he got the principal's job, he stopped dropping by, stopped calling for advice or just to shoot the breeze. He moved on to a different place filled with different priorities and allegiances. It's probably just a matter of time before he forgets.

But let me tell you about this other student teacher I had. I remember everything about this poor soul except his first name. There's probably some symbolism in that, but when you're retired you don't have to look for it any more.

His name was Roseday. The kids called him Nosegay. He showed up his first day wearing a tan corduroy jacket, a blue shirt, and a green striped tie. I remember that vividly because he wore the same clothes every day for almost three weeks. I could tell from his lunch that the kid didn't have much money. So I bought him a jacket and a shirt and gave him some of my old ties. He didn't know how to knot them so I did it for him. All he had to do was pull them over his head.

He was clueless about kids...and grammar...and literature. I always let student teachers pick their first unit of study. I figured if they liked it, they'd do a good job.

"What's your favorite?" I asked him.

"Poetry," said he with eyes averted. He was shy.

"Favorite poets?"

"Emily Dickinson."

"Oh Christ!" I thought. "Of all the poets on earth, not Emily Dickinson!" I was of the opinion then and now that Emily's stuff should have been kept in her trunk in perpetuity. The only way to get through her doggerel was to *sing* it to the tune of *The Yellow Rose of Texas*.

Here—try it:

> I taste a liquor never brewed—
> From Tankards scooped in Pearl—
> Not all the Vats upon the Rhine
> Yield such an Alcohol!

I know, I know. You're thinking it should be *alcohurl*, right?

My disdain for Dickinson was the only personal opinion I ever voiced in my classroom. Kids never knew if I were Democrat or Republican, pro-abortion or pro-life, for or against the death penalty, prayers in school, dress codes, legalization of pot—you name the controversy. They never could be sure where I stood. Some guy named F.W. Robertson had this to say:

> "The true aim of every one who aspires to be a teacher should be, not to impart his own opinions, but to kindle minds."

(I found this in one of my two all-time favorite books—*The New Dictionary of Thoughts*. The other is *Jude the Obscure*.)

Like Robertson, whoever the hell he was, I believed it was my job to get kids to think about what *they* believed and to ask themselves *why* they believed it. They got enough propaganda from their social studies teachers; they didn't need more from me. But they knew where I stood on Emily.

"Dickinson is a fine choice," I lied. I didn't want to disappoint Roseday who was showing the first burst of passion I had seen since he showed up. I was teaching eleventh grade then—American lit—the best grade to teach because the kids were still semi-serious about their education, especially those going off to college. I turned one of those classes over to Mr. Roseday.

"Good afternoon," he said so quietly no one responded. It didn't help that he was facing the blackboard at the time writing EMILY DICKSON on it. He turned to the class and asked them to tell him what they knew about her. Well, all they knew was the awful stuff I had said about her and they were smart enough to keep that to themselves. All except Andrew. He was the nitpicker, the faultfinder. Every teacher knows the type and every teacher wants to smack him.

"I know that she spelled her name Dick-**IN**-son," said Andrew. "And Mr. Angelo says her poetry sucks."

In my defense I never said *sucks*…in front of the class. I averted Roseday's eyes but gave Andrew a double dose of *mal occhi*.

Things did not go well. His lesson was thirty minutes short of the forty-eight minute period. Everything he wrote on the board he misspelled. Everything he said he mispronounced. He said "ono mata *pway* uh" and when the kids laughed, he said it again. He knew there was a joke in there somewhere; he just didn't know *he* was it. In desperation he told them to begin their homework. Of course he forgot to assign them any.

It was becoming painfully apparent that teaching was not his calling. He had the desire, but he lacked the talent. I worked with him on his lesson plans. I shared games and activities with him. I timed his lessons. I taught him how to ask open-ended questions, but when he stood before the class, he literally disappeared. It was sad to watch. Then one day he didn't show up. He didn't call. Nothing. I was worried. I had a horrible vision of this kid killing himself. I called his home. The phone rang and rang and rang. Finally it was answered. "Hello? Hello? Hello?" I got no response. "Can you hear me?"

"Yes." It was almost whispered.

"It's Mr. Angelo."

"I know."

"I was worried about you. Are you all right?"

"I can't do it." His voice cracked.

"Want to try again tomorrow? We can work on plans and delivery."

"What's the use? I can't do it."

I had a vision of this kid sitting on the floor next to his ringing phone with a razor blade in his hand as he stared at his exposed wrist. That's the kind of shit you think of when you see too many movies. Holden Caulfield was right about that too.

He didn't kill himself and he didn't come back to my school or his college. He dropped out and faded away. My students didn't even ask where he was. My colleagues blamed me. It was the department joke: Tony got rid of another one.

"Did you scare this one off too?" The reference was to the last semester's student teacher who went to the men's room after teaching a pitiful lesson on pronouns. He never came back. This one did call though—from a payphone around the corner. "I can't do it." That's all he said.

It took a lot for both of these guys to admit incompetence. I was surrounded by teachers who couldn't do it either, but that never stopped *them*. Some couldn't do it for over twenty-five years. They're the ones who gave the rest of us black eyes. And it was now time for me and my black eyes to leave.

How does a forty-year career end? Very quietly and very lonely. I surveyed room 112 for the last time in June, 2004. It was my home away from home for decades. It felt like it was mine—although most years I shared it with other teachers. In fact, it's the rare high school teacher who has a room to call his very own. The ones that do probably have photos of their principals in compromising positions. But for the rest of us it's the old assembly line of public education. "All done? Get out! Next!"

I looked up at the ceiling. It was the poor man's Sistine Chapel. Once a month I asked kids to adapt a short story on our required list to another form. It could be a poem, a news article, an ad, a play, a video—whatever. One kid many years ago asked if she could paint her adaptation. I said yes. "On the ceiling?" I said yes again. I didn't ask anybody for permission. I had *assumptive authority*. I just assumed I could do anything to get my subject across in the most enjoyable way. In my early years it often got me in trouble with principals. In my later years I was king, albeit self-proclaimed. I did whatever the hell I wanted.

And so the young lady removed a ceiling tile—probably laden with deadly asbestos—and brought it back three days later with her colorful interpretation of "A Rose for Emily" by William Faulkner. She had painted a double bed seen through a sheer curtain with an indentation of a head on one of the pillows. There was a single strand of gray hair on that pillow, but you couldn't see it from the floor. You'd have to stand on a desk and crane your neck. Nitpicker Andrew did just that to verify the accuracy of his classmate's rendition. In the bottom left corner was a long-stemmed red rose. Forming a semi-circle were the words *A Rose for Emily*. I gave her an A...which gave the other kids over the years the impetus to emulate the Italian masters.

There was a catcher's mitt up there, its pocket loaded with poems—at least one of them a sleazy limerick. It was Allie's, Holden Caulfield's dead brother. Next to that was a building bearing the sign Intellectual Brothel. Leaning provocatively against the front door was a curvaceous blonde wearing a Phi Beta Kappa key in her cleavage. She was holding *The Iliad* in one hand, *Paradise Lost* in the other. It was a clever adaptation of Woody Allen's "The Whore of Mensa". A mound of bloodstained rocks for Shirley Jackson's "The Lottery" brought a wave of equally macabre depictions of Poe's "The Tell-Tale Heart" and Stephen King's "The Bogeyman".

Chaz, the nicest kid God ever created, was not the sharpest pencil in the box. But he wanted in on painting ceiling tiles. His class was reading a novel—*Third and Indiana*. "That's not a short story, Chaz."

"So?"

So indeed. If Chaz wanted to paint a tile, so be it. "Okay, Chaz. Go for it. But be sure to include a street sign so everyone will know what it's supposed to represent."

"Duh, Ranj. Who don't know that?!" I smiled as I looked up at his rendering. There was a tattooed tough leaning against a street sign that read 'Thirdandindiana.' Not separately. All one word. Chaz, I'm sure will go to his dying day believing that Third and Indiana was the name of *one* street. But the pride he took in that tile was heart-warming. He actually came back the year after his graduation to see if it were still there.

There were twenty-five painted tiles in all. And when they ran out of room, they asked about painting on the walls. For years I said no. Then two kids asked if they could paint a memorial mural. I asked for a sketch. They gave me one. I approved it.

Three weeks later after hours of after-school work they unveiled their masterpiece. It was a graveyard with several old tombstones bearing the titles of books the kids hated. The largest stone bore *The Scarlet Letter*. Off to the far left was the most garish headstone. A vulture perched atop it held a *Warriner's English Grammar and Composition* book in its bent beak…on the stone:

RIP
Mr. Angelo

I walked over to the bookcase—8 feet long—that I brought from home. I got tired requisitioning one so I just made my own. It was lopsided. Everything I built was lopsided, but if you jammed six Phillies baseball cards under the right back leg, it was perfect. As I packed things away I could hear my wife: "Don't bring home lots of junk."

But the *junk* was so neat. I just couldn't trash it. There was my Marilyn Monroe collection. When teaching *Death of a Salesman* I mentioned in passing that Miller was married to Marilyn, my first love. That's when the pictures and postcards started coming in. One Christmas a class gave me a tie depicting Marilyn trying to hold down her white dress over the blasting steam vent. Remember that one? For my birthday they gave me an old Teachers On Strike sign that they had adorned with blown up photos—one of the voluptuous MM with slightly parted lips and the other of a younger, eyeglass-less, wrinkle-less, and grayless AAA. It had two captions:

Some Like It Tepid.

and

Grammar Is A Girl's Best Friend!

Another year a class gave me a flag with a busty Marilyn superimposed on the field of stars. It was too risqué to be unfurled so it was kept folded on the shelf…next to the blonde wig. The wig was often used as a prop for plays whether appropriate or not.

There was my gavel with "Tony" painted on it. A kid made it for me because he thought it was unsightly for me to rap my knuckles on my rusty gray-metal speaker's stand. My LIKE jar. It was empty now but it was usually full of nickels gleaned from careless speakers who like said like whenever like they couldn't like think of like anything else to like say. I'd stand out in the hall before class and select a kid to be the day's Tax Collector. I usually picked the loud mouth who never shut up, the one who never gave the other kids a chance to say anything, the one who never raised his hand…just blurted stuff out. I gave him this slip:

> **Congratulations! You are today's Tax Collector. Listen carefully to everything said by ALL speakers. Be especially alert to the word LIKE…every time you hear it used incorrectly or as nothing more than filler, tax the speaker 5 cents. At the end of the period report your findings to the class, collect the money and put it in the "LIKE" jar, and return this paper to the teacher, a former IRS Agent.**

Once a month I'd take the nickels to the nearby Entenmann Bakery Outlet and buy anything that cost a dollar a box. I tried to go on Wednesdays, Senior Citizen Day, to get an additional 10% off. If you happened to be there when the van from the nursing home was dropping off folks, you'd get an extra 15%. I was not above pretending to be a *resident*. Sometimes I even limped.

There was a box full of VHS cassettes from the Public Speaking classes. Every kid was to tape every presentation so he could plot his own progress toward stardom. But some kids left them behind. How could I throw them away? There were kids I knew on them. And all the trays and Tupperware containers that still held rock-hard crumbs of the last class party. I just started at one end and went to the other, sweeping everything into my take-home box.

I did the same with the photographs that filled the bulletin board behind my desk. Scores of kids from scores of years stared back at me. Some at their desks, some on the field or on the court. I thought I'd put them in a scrapbook some day.

I looked at the shelf that held the VCR, my *own* VCR, because again I got weary requisitioning one. "If I got you one, I'd have to get everyone else one," said the fair-minded Paper Asshole.

"Good idea," I countered. "Every teacher *should* have one." He smiled and walked away. So I bought my own. Screw him. I had a coupon.

There was a folder full of newspaper clippings I kept of my students' accomplishments in school and out. Some were clippings about *me* that kids cut out of the local paper and brought in to discuss or berate. The one on top was yellowed with age but the subject was still current.

A Look at the Teacher Strikes in Pennsylvania

I remember that it frayed a nerve and prompted an Angelo response:

Dear Editor:

Your "look at the teacher strikes in Penna." is cross-eyed at least and wall-eyed at best.

Your opinions, however myopic, are consistent with other anti-union ones made over the years unless, of course, that union happens to be the Pa. School Boards Association.

The simple truth is that you and the community at large care little about public education and public school educators. Why else would you write: "at one time teachers were expected to set an example for those whom they taught. It's hardly that way today."

I am up to my armpits with those who cry "Example! Set a good example!" Who teaches the child profanity, prejudice, discrimination, and disrespect. Not the public school teacher.

Who supplies the child with cigarette money, drug money, and dirty book and movie money? Not the public school teacher.

Please begin pointing your editorial fingers at parents—parents who bear children and then can't 'bear' them; parents who allow kids to violate curfews and then scream at the school's permissiveness; parents who preach black or white supremacy and then claim the schools instigate racial incidents; parents who want the very best in education as long as it costs them very little.

Consider all this the next time you're tempted to ask: "How is it possible to rear children who will have respect for the laws of our country when they see teachers defying them...?"

"Good one, Mr. Angelo," said one of my students. "My dad said you should get a *REAL* job."

"Good one, Tony," said my wife. "That's sure to increase our volume of hate mail."

Looking back I'm thinking I could write the same letter today. Nothing's changed. They are still out there—the mean-spirited motley militia of educational minutia armed with brickbats and vouchers chartering schools like there's no tomorrow. Pity the teachers who continue to stand out there in the great abyss of state and national rules and regulations designed to choke out creativity and strangle self-realization.

I can't help thinking that this mess is all my fault. When I started teaching in 1964, the SAT's began their decline. I take full responsibility for lower scores—math and verbal—drug addicts, unwed mothers, child molesters (remember, I'm Catholic), the war in Iraq, soaring gasoline prices, and infant mortality. I am sorry for these and all the sins I cannot remember.

Kids. I miss kids. But I'm getting over it. There's nothing else about the job that makes any sense. The state and nation see to it regularly that the educational process is rife with bullshit. Test, Threaten, and Humiliate—that should be the motto of the Department of Education.

Now I just smile and nod like the smart kids in the front row as I read two morning newspapers and ride eight miles on my stationary bike. I eat when I am hungry and go to the bathroom whenever I want. I nap in between. Life is good.

And when I get a little nostalgic for my other life, I'll open up that box of junk and read the cards and letters from the only folks that count—the kids.

I've shared enough and you've read enough. And so as I told my students at the end of every class period—thanks for stopping by.

Today's Freewrite…

"Hey kid! Yeah you! Get off my grass!"

978-0-595-40619-7
0-595-40619-X

Printed in the United States
93949LV00004B/271-276/A